CW01513097

THE
BILLIONAIRE
AND HIS
SCANDAL

paige press

THE BILLIONAIRE AND HIS SCANDAL

SADIE BLACK

Copyright © 2022 by Sadie Black

All rights reserved.

No part of this book may be reproduced in any form or by any electronic or mechanical means, including information storage and retrieval systems, without written permission from the author, except for the use of brief quotations in a book review.

Paige Press
Leander, TX 78641

Ebook:
ISBN: 978-1-953520-95-1

Print:
ISBN: 978-1-957647-25-8

Also by Sadie Black

HIS NANNY TRILOGY

The Billionaire and His Nanny

The Billionaire and His Scandal

The Billionaire and His Forever

About This Book

When Abbie Montgomery arrived, I knew she would destroy me.
My best friend's daughter, virginal and still harboring her childhood crush on me, was completely off-limits.

Of course, forbidden desires are always the sweetest. Watching her bond with my daughter during the day, giving into sweet, soft temptation at night... I always knew it couldn't last. I always knew it would end badly. But I never expected the spark between us could explode my entire life

Chapter One

Graham

THERE's an old British phrase my father was particularly fond of: the cock-up. Its roots are deeply contested, though the Scottish king himself, Robert Burns, used it in flowery form. Cock up your hat, cock up your arms, cock up your gun, cock feathers. My father, the puritan he was, said it was meant as a warning: *prepare yourself*.

"Cock up, my boy. We're going out," he would say. "Cock up, lad, danger is coming."

I can hear his warning echoing in my mind, thundering around the dome of my brain, stabbing its way down my spine.

Cock up, old boy. Trouble is brewing.

Where was his warning two weeks ago? A month ago? Should I have known better, my entire life a preparatory course for this very moment? His lessons remained in the background for most of my life, and only now—when it's indubitably too late—do they come to the forefront again to provide guidance.

"Cock up, Graham," I mutter, my voice taut.

I'm fucking furious. It's all I can do to stand here with my features schooled into stoicism while Abbie sits frozen before me, a sheen of tears in her eyes. No doubt wallowing in self-pity.

As though this entire fucking fiasco impacted only her.

What the hell was I thinking? Every step of the way was littered with red flags and neon warning signs and yet I ignored all of them, and for what? To get my rocks off?

The rolled-up tabloids burn a hole in my clenched fist, but I can't bring myself to set them down. Right now, they are my anchor. My tether. Without them clutched in my hand, I will fly apart. Ironically, it is their very existence that is threatening to undo me.

"Graham, please." Abbie's voice is soft and pathetic. It's childish, it's timid, lacking the fire I lusted after. It makes me wonder if the spark I saw in her was ever there at all. "I didn't—"

Her words split the stone wall blocking off my fraught emotions and split them into countless fractals. Rage overtakes me, like fingers around my throat, my stomach, my balls, squeezing until I can see and feel nothing but the fury.

"You didn't?" The words come roaring out like a tsunami. "You didn't what, exactly? Because frankly, all of these?" I rip the first tabloid out of my hand and throw it down in front of her. She winces, which only stokes the fire inside me even further. I take the second one and slam it on my desk under my fist, a thunderclap against the heavy oak. "These say you *did*."

"I don't know wh—"

"Enough!" I slam another one down. And another. And another. Each one accompanied by another thud of my palm, hitting the oak surface with a force stronger than before. Framed photos of my daughter shake, just one more precious piece of my life impacted by her lies.

Meanwhile, all Abbie can manage is a look of shock. Which is undoubtedly an act—unless it's that she's somehow surprised by my reaction to her betrayal.

The magazine on top of the pile blares its ugly head-line from the desk between us, the incriminating photo below it grainy from being enlarged, a scene from Jude's recent riding exhibition. The angle makes it look like Abbie and I are clandestinely sharing lovers' secrets while seated next to Natasha, painting my deceit as grotesque and furtive and palpable. In a series of smaller shots below, I'm merely handing Abbie a cup of lemon-ade, a rare smile on my face, but the act looks so much more despicable under the coarse lens of the paparazzi.

"Nanny Confesses All," I read aloud. The words slide out cold and hard and as dangerous as I feel. "Does she, now?"

"Graham—"

"Don't." Another tabloid slams down, rattling a crystal bourbon glass on the desk. "Graham Ratliff Finding Relief in the Help?" I snarl. This one hits partic-ularly hard, for reasons I can't quite place.

I go on. "Nannygate—that's clever, isn't it?"

I slam the next one even harder, my fist starting to ache. "Billionaire Banker Seduces Teenage Nanny—The Scandal Explodes." This particular photo is harder to place, darker and less clear than the others. It looks like the inside of a bar, but it can't be, because she's underage.

And then I remember that night, weeks ago, searching for her all over town, on the prowl, checking each bar for her instead of staying home to entertain my intended, more age-appropriate companion. I used to pride myself on being a man of level-headed thinking and sound rationale. All of that appears to have gone out the fucking window when it comes to this woman—no, this girl—seated before me.

"Ratliff Affair with Barely Legal Nanny," I read, dropping another onto the pile and giving the whole mess another heavy pound of my angry fist.

With that, the crystal glass falls off the edge of the desk and shatters on the floor. I almost laugh, adrenaline flooding my veins and a hit of endorphins cascading through me.

I crumple the last tabloid in my fist, crushing our faces together, and then hurl it at the wall. It hits with a soft thwack and falls to the floor. Disappointing, oddly. Hardly a match for the explosive feelings roiling in my gut.

"Was this all some sort of fucking game to you?" I roar, turning my gaze back to Abbie.

"No," she murmurs weakly. Her blue eyes are wide and innocent, but I know it's a farce.

Venom pumps through my veins and my fists tingle at my sides, but that is where they will remain. Because I cannot—will not—ever raise a hand to a woman; I cannot simply grab Abbie in one hand and crush her like I did the disgusting pages of the trashy tabloids that spell out my undoing. My complete and utter destruction, both personally and professionally.

Besides, touching Abbie has caused enough problems already. It's something I'll never do again.

"Then what the hell were you thinking, selling me out like that? Did you need the money that badly? I don't pay you enough, I suppose? Or were you expecting extra for the additional *services* you provided?" I sneer.

"Please, you have to believe me." Her voice comes out choked, laden with the guilty tears of someone caught red-handed. "I didn't tell anyone about...us."

"Bullshit. How did this leak, then? How did these details flood the news overnight?"

Abbie shakes her head. "I really don't know."

"Oh no?" I shove the magazines around until I find the one that reads NANNY CONFESSES ALL, and I hold it up for her to see. "You're telling me I have another nanny?"

"Graham, listen, please. It wasn't me!"

"You. Are. Lying," I grind out. She has to be, regardless of how genuine her protests might seem. "You think I don't know a thing or two about actresses?" I laugh incredulously. "Did you forget, in your quest to dominate my household, that I was formerly married to one?"

"I didn't go to the press. I didn't sell you out. I swear." Her voice rests just above a whisper. "This isn't an act."

Nope. Not buying it. I lived with this kind of shit for years with Natasha, the protests and pleading and declarations of fidelity made directly to my face, but meanwhile she was fucking whoever she wanted behind my back and feigning innocence when she was called out on it.

"What have you done?" I spit the words out.

I'm not just referring to the tabloid leak, either. What was her true purpose in coming to the estate to begin with? Now that her deception is out in the open, it throws her entire presence here into question.

"I—I—" But she can't get the words out. Her tears start to fall and she covers her face with her hands, playing up her youthful innocence. She's so good, I almost feel sorry for her.

The urge to smash something else against the wall takes hold of me, but before I have a chance to grab anything else in the office, the phone rings.

Not my business phone.

My personal cell phone. The one only about three people have the number for.

Pure adrenaline trickles through my veins. Without even checking, I know exactly who it is. I toss my laptop back on the desk and point to the door.

"Get out."

Abbie doesn't have to be told twice. She stumbles to her feet and hustles out of the room, hair streaming behind her. Good riddance.

I grab the phone and jab at the green icon, closing my eyes as I lift it to my ear. "What do you want, Natasha?"

"Oh, Graham. Don't play stupid. You know exactly what I want," my ex-wife all but purrs.

My blood runs cold. "I'm not interested in your games."

"This isn't a game, darling." The poison she's sending

down the line cuts straight through me. "This is about the protection and well-being of my young, impressionable daughter."

"*Our* daughter."

"*My* daughter. You're clearly too busy screwing the help to think about what's best for her," the ice queen hisses, and it's like I can actually hear the smile in her voice.

"Screwing? Really?" I pace around my office, trying and failing to regain some semblance of calm. "Are we children now?"

"I didn't realize you cared so much about vernacular when it came to fucking your nanny. Is that better, darling? Is *fucking* a better word to describe what you're doing?"

I grab a flame-shaped glass trophy I received from the board when our company officially crossed the billion-dollar mark. It carries a nice weight in my hands as I debate smashing it into the wall. "This doesn't concern you."

"It absolutely concerns me. And my sweet Jude. Which is why my lawyer will be in touch with yours before the end of day to formally demand I get full custody."

"Never."

She laughs. "You can't fight me on this and win, Graham. You've already proven that you can't take care of her yourself by hiring a damn nanny to begin with, and now you're too preoccupied fucking that teenage tart to properly care for Judey at all. I'll be coming to collect her this afternoon and I expect her things to be packed."

"That's not how this works, Tash." I swallow down the fury in my throat and try to channel the stoic, collected front that I require for engaging with her.

"Don't 'Tash' me," she snaps. "I didn't call for your excuses or your bullshit or your sorry-ass attempt at intimidation tactics. I called for my daughter. And you will hand her over before I light your ass up everywhere. You think this will stop at the tabloids? We both know a judge won't look kindly on this. And as for your nanny, you better thank your lucky stars she hasn't tried to publicly #metoo your ass. Yet."

I freeze mid-pace as her words wash over me. I can't even argue. Because she's fucking right. The entire country now believes I'm the kind of father who takes advantage of his kid's teenaged nanny. And they aren't exactly wrong, are they? Jesus.

"You are an absent, self-absorbed workaholic of a father, and Jude deserves better," Natasha goes on. "You don't even deserve the *chance* to care for someone as precious and pure as Jude. You had a responsibility to protect her, and you failed."

Under normal circumstances, I can dodge her venom easily, but this time her terrible words hit me right in the gut. They're not just her usual harsh barbs. They're all my worst fears, realized. I am a shit father. I've let my child down. And I have no idea how to fix it.

I swallow down a knot in my throat and give the award another toss in my hand. "I'm not handing over custody without a formal order."

"Fine. I won't have any trouble getting one and you

know it, Graham. This is just a stalling tactic. I'm not bluffing."

"Nor am I." I hang up without waiting for her response. And then I pitch the award across the room, watching it shatter with a sick satisfaction.

My footsteps echo through the house like thunder as I storm to the west wing. I want Abbie to know I'm coming. I want her to be fearful. I want her to understand the depth of fuckery she committed. I am a stone's throw away from losing everything I hold dear. And all for what, a piece of ass?

How was any of this worth it?

I very nearly put a hole in her door as I bang on it, and then throw it open without waiting for her response. Abbie is crumpled in a heap on the bed, mascara streaked down her face.

"You. I want you gone forever from my sight and my house. Start making arrangements for your departure. You are relieved of your duties, effective immediately."

"No. Please," Abbie stutters between sobs.

"Immediately," I repeat.

With that, I turn on my heel and slam the door shut behind me.

Chapter Two

Abbie

THIS CAN'T BE REAL. It can't be.

The words loop through my brain endlessly, echoing in my mind as I stare up at the ceiling through wet eyes. Everything was so perfect, everything was going exactly as I needed it to, and then it all fell apart.

How the hell did this happen?

Just yesterday, everything was right in the world. A mere twenty-four hours ago, Graham held me, caressed me, kissed me, cared for me. We made love like a real couple. We walked, talked, and behaved like two people in a solid, albeit new, relationship. And now this.

In the blink of an eye, it all came crashing down. Who did this? And when? And why?

My heart hurts, my stomach clenched, a crushing weight in my chest. Air flees my lungs like Graham fled our relationship. I can barely breathe as I lay curled in a ball on my bed, praying that when I finally gain the strength to get up again, the world will look differently.

But I know it won't.

Even if Graham doesn't believe me, I know I didn't do it. I wouldn't have. But it doesn't matter, because someone else fucked everything up for us—and Graham forgot everything he knew about me the instant those incriminating headlines appeared.

My phone rings, playing the ringtone designated for when my dad calls. He's going to be livid and I know I have to answer, but I can't bring myself to take the call. I just want to stay here not moving, avoiding reality as long as I can and pretending I don't exist.

My relationship with Graham was a complicated one, yes, but at least it existed. We had finally been spending quality time together as a couple after weeks (if not years) of me dreaming and scheming and planning and somehow actually falling in love with him and his handsome, stupid face. And it all shattered in one devastating moment.

The worst part might be that Graham thinks I'm a liar. That I was lying all along. He accused me of "acting," and compared me to Natasha, his vile ex-wife. As if I'm truly no better than that conniving, manipulative bitch as far as he's concerned.

He hates me.

The thought leaves me feeling gutted and hollow. How can he actually believe that none of what we had was even real? I've worked so hard to get him to trust me, to open up, to fall for me, and when he was finally in my grasp? Boom. Decimated. Destroyed. Obliviated. Forever.

My phone rings again, playing the same annoying song. I need to change it. I need to silence it. I need my dad to go away and leave me to rot in peace. But I know he won't stop calling until I answer, so I finally reach for my phone on the nightstand and pick up.

"Hello?"

"What the hell happened?" His voice is harsh and grating in my ear. "Abbie, Jesus Christ! What the fuck?"

"I didn't do it." I can't stop the tears from spilling down again, hot and stinging the already-raw skin of my cheeks. "I swear, it wasn't me."

"Oh no? What other nanny does Graham Ratliff have, then?"

"You sound just like him," I whisper, his words like barbs under my skin. "That's exactly what he said."

"Of course he did, because he's not an idiot," Dad snaps. "But I'm starting to think you are."

His words shouldn't hurt me as much as they do, but I can't stop the fresh torrent of tears. I try to muffle my cries and stuttering breaths with my hand, shuddering at the pressure of everything that's weighing down on me, but the sounds escape my chapped lips anyway.

"Are you crying?" Dad asks, his voice softening. "Abbie, talk to me. What happened?"

"He hates me!" The words pour out in a wail. "God, everything was so perfect and then someone must have found out and told the press, and now Graham hates me. He told me to leave and never come back."

"Is this a surprise?" Dad scoffs. "I can't blame the man. You ruined him. And you ruined him before we were ready."

"I didn't d-do it..." I insist. Nobody believes me, not

even my own father. "And now I'll never s-see him again." A fresh sob rips through me.

"Jesus. I don't believe this." Dad exhales slowly. "Abigail Eileen Montgomery, did you lose your head when you went up there and fucking *fall* for him?"

I can't make myself deny it, but I squeeze my eyes shut and clamp a hand over my mouth, my face red hot, struggling to keep the hurricane of emotions bottled up. I'm devastated and angry and grieving and hurt. But I can't let my dad know I ruined our plan even worse than it already is. I can't let him know the truth.

"Fuck. You did. You really fell for him." He sighs heavily. "This was not part of the plan, little girl."

Swiping a handful of tissues from the box on my bed, I blot ineffectually at my eyes. Still, I say nothing. My words are trapped inside me, slicing me to pieces.

"Idiot. This really throws a fucking wrench in the works." His words come out tense, breathless. But not defeated. "Okay. It is what it is. Guess I'll just have to fix it, then."

"Dad—"

"Don't, Abigail," he snaps. "You've done enough. You assured me you could do this. You spent weeks dodging my calls and my texts, refusing all my help, swearing you could handle this. And look what happened."

"I just—"

"Stop. I don't want to hear it. I don't know what I was thinking, trusting you with something like this. This is *my* fault," he says, disgusted.

"I didn't tell anyone!" I yell, surprising myself. "I

don't know who threw us under the bus, but I did exactly what I was supposed to do!"

"Bullshit. You forgot yourself. You went up there and acted like a lovesick schoolgirl and at some point you clearly got careless. You forgot everything I taught you. Everything I sent you there to do. It doesn't matter whether you went to the press directly or not—you let this happen." His anger isn't as hot as Graham's, but it burns me all the same. "This wasn't the plan, Abs. You were supposed to save the family."

Hot anger throbs in my temples, enough to finally still my tears. "Well, sorry to have disappointed you and ruined all your plans, but I'm fired now. So I guess I'll just have to seduce someone else," I snap.

I'm going for bitter sarcasm, but it just comes out sounding sad and pathetic. My dad is right—I am an idiot. I did fall for Graham. I ignored what I was supposed to do and let my emotions get the best of me and in the end, it blew up in my face. There's nothing I can do about it now, except mourn the loss of what could have been.

I never should have agreed to help my dad. I should have listened to that tiny voice in the back of my head that said it was never going to work. Hindsight is a bitch.

"Seduce *someone else*?" Dad repeats. "Not if I have anything to say about it." The anger is gone from his voice, replaced by a familiar tone. The one he uses when he's dreaming up schemes. "Stop sniveling and feeling sorry for yourself and get back to doing your Lolita act again. I'm going to fix this. I'll see you soon."

He hangs up without another word. I stare at the

phone for a moment, letting my vision blur as the sadness wrecks me again.

Forcing myself to get up, I pad to the bathroom to blow my nose and splash cool water on my face but pull up short at the sight of my pitiful reflection. My hair is a mess, my eyes red-rimmed and bloodshot, my face puffy, mascara streaks everywhere. I'm a fucking mess.

"Dad is his best friend," I whisper to myself. "He'll fix this. He'll know what to say."

Graham won't be able to deny my father—not when he's carrying the guilt of having slept with me over the last few weeks of my nannying gig and the two of them have got a history way older than my small set of years. Besides, my dad can get anyone to do anything. I've seen it with my own eyes. If anyone can fix this, he can.

I wash my face with renewed purpose and brush my teeth afterward for good measure. Then I spend a few minutes on my hair, growing calmer by the minute. Maybe not everything is lost. Dad will tell Graham I'm innocent. He'll tell him that I would never betray him, and Graham will listen to him. He has to. That's what best friends are for, right?

Amanda calls just then, like a guardian angel from above, as if she knew I needed her in this exact moment. I take a deep, shaky breath before I answer.

"Hello?" My voice cracks and I have to take another deep breath.

"Oh, honey," Amanda gushes. "I saw all the news. I am so sorry. Are you okay?"

No one, not even my father, asked me if I was okay. I've been yelled at, accused of things I didn't do, and cast out by the only man that matters to me, and no one stopped to ask me if I was okay. Those three little words break me and I dissolve into tears.

"It's okay," Amanda soothes through the receiver. "Let it out. I can't imagine what you're going through."

"I don't know what to do," I whisper. "It wasn't me. I didn't go to the press."

"I know. I know you'd never."

"Everything was so perfect." I choke on a small sob. "We were going to be *together*, Amanda. For real. And it barely lasted a day before those fucking headlines hit."

"Do you know who ratted you out?" she asks.

"Not for sure, but I have my suspicions." I chew my lip, hashing over what I know about Esmeralda. It has to be her.

When I first arrived at the Ratliff estate, she was incredibly kind to me. I thought we were friends, even. The more attention I got from Graham, however, the icier she became. The more snide comments I caught from her. And who else had such an unobstructed front-row seat to the relationship blossoming between me and her boss?

The highs and lows flash in my mind, unbidden and impossible to forget. The first time Graham fingered me across his desk, giving me the most mind-blowing orgasm of my life—the first of many. As soon as I came, he unceremoniously tossed me out of his office, like I meant nothing to him. I remember wanting Esmeralda to comfort me so badly, to tell me men were terrible and I deserved better. But she did no such thing, because she didn't know about it.

Or so I thought.

And then there was the time he pulled my pants down in the middle of the woods and fucked my ass cheeks. We were all alone out there in the forest. Weren't we?

Did she know about the night he stalked me around town, when I went out dressed to kill, and nearly got himself into a fight with the college boy I was dancing with? Did she know I lured the stable boy, Quinn, into taking me out on a date just to enrage Graham with jealousy? No.

But she did see the way I retaliated against the terrible schoolgirl-esque uniform Graham gave me, in one of his many attempts to control me, by slutting it up. And she had to have noticed the way I liked to wear revealing clothing around my boss. She definitely hadn't seemed to approve of that much at all, always casting judgmental glances my way.

Still, it's hard to believe she'd betray Graham like this. If she didn't like me, she could have just pressed him to fire me and find someone else. Maybe she did and he refused to listen?

Fear suddenly tickles my belly. Up until this point, I haven't stopped to really think about who else might have told. I was too busy trying to plead my innocence to men who didn't want to listen. But the truth is, I'd told others about me and Graham, too. Cassie, Jude's riding instructor. Quinn, the stable hand. Amanda herself. That was it though, wasn't it?

"I always thought tabloids were pure bullshit," I tell Amanda. "I thought everyone knew they were garbage, just shit made up for entertainment value. Why does no one believe me?"

"Probably because it's true?" Amanda says gently. "But yes, those magazines are full of crap most of the time. You're right about that. You've just got to convince Graham that the headlines are just a bunch of rumors from some asshole who doesn't want to see you two happy together. Ooh, wait! What if it was his ex-wife? Half of these pictures have Natasha in them somewhere. What if she was trying to take the spotlight off her own affairs?"

"Oh my God, you genius." The tears dry up in my eyes, heart racing, mind whirling. "You fucking genius. I'll bet it *was* her. Natasha hates me. You should see the way she looks at me every time she comes over. She always made little comments about Graham and me, too."

"What's that thing people say about the simplest answer being the correct one?"

"Occam's razor," I supply.

"Well there you go. Think about it. It's always the domestic partner. Her jealousy is, like, notorious, and you're taking care of her kid and spending all your time with her man," Amanda says sensibly. "In fact, I bet she showed up at Jude's riding exhibition just to arrange those photos for when she blabbed all over to the press."

Wow. I should be more upset, but this revelation soothes me. It has to be Natasha. It totally makes sense. Esmeralda wouldn't have done this. And Cassie is my friend.

"Graham hates her," I say. "I just need some solid

evidence that she was the one who did this, and I'll be back in his good graces."

"Girl, if anyone can prove their innocence, it's you. You've got this."

"Thank you."

After I hang up, I fling open the closet doors and start rifling around for an outfit that I know Graham likes. Nervous energy hums through my veins. If my dad can talk him out of firing me, maybe we can convince him that this was all just a shitty publicity stunt by his ex-wife, and I'll be back in his arms in no time.

Amanda's right, I tell myself. *I've got this.*

Chapter Three

Graham

Sunlight streams through my office windows, illuminating the piles of work I've left unattended. Instead of poring over spreadsheets and fielding calls, I've stared at the awards and photographic evidence of momentous occasions lining my walls, wondering where it all went pear shaped.

I've spent most of my life dedicated to business, to being a decent man, to being both efficacious and prosperous. I've been successful at those things for as long as I can remember, a byproduct of years of learning and luck and, more often than not, exceptionally hard work. The results all sit here, in this room, where I should feel like a king.

Instead, I'm very much a pauper.

Everything went to shit when Natasha left me (and Jude) for her litany of lovers, but the media frenzy mostly left me unscathed. I've been known through the years as a philanthropist, a family man, a doting father. So when the press got their hands on the story of Natasha's infidelity, they mostly portrayed her as a troublesome celebrity actress. Meanwhile, the few negative headlines about me never bothered me much, in part because they were so obviously one-sided, but also because the triviality of it all was beneath me. Who cares what some cellar dweller had to say about the status of my marriage?

I didn't get to where I am now by listening to the whims and lies of those chasing a venomous coin. If I did, I'd still be in my father's mailroom, sorting mail and trash into bins and dreaming of greater things. But I knew I could do better than that, go farther and reach higher, and thus I elevated. So why does this recent nastiness cut so deep?

The truth buzzes around my ears like a hornet and I swat it away, a nuisance to be avoided at all costs.

My second glass of scotch feels as heavy as the nonsense crushing my shoulders. This is not becoming. My father is likely turning in his grave right now, though he, too, had a penchant for young women. I suppose I would have made him proud—until I didn't.

Outside, I can see Abbie playing with Jude in the pool. She's still here, waiting for her father to pick her up from the estate. I didn't tell her to spend time with my daughter; I said her duties were relieved. Yet here she is, attending to my child. Attending to Jude's needs in ways I haven't. In ways I can't at the moment—because my efforts to stay away from Abbie have resulted in me pushing away Jude as well.

God, Abbie still looks like the innocent little doll whose virginity I claimed, but I know better now. She's nothing but a snake in doll's clothes. Why is it that the women in my life always ruin everything? Meanwhile Jude's getting older, and she'll probably take her turn soon enough. Sooner still with every moment she spends close to Abbie.

My hands clench around the glass tumbler, too heavy to crush under the weight of my fury. Pity.

A firm hand knocks twice on my door, pauses, and knocks thrice more. I swallow down the rest of my drink and stare into the bottom of the glass, wishing there were answers there.

"Enter," I say, expecting Esmeralda.

The door carefully opens, though I don't turn in my chair to greet my housekeeper. I can hear her inhale sharply as she surveys the extent of the damage. I haven't yet cleaned up the mess from my earlier exchange with Miss Montgomery.

Even the thought of her name stirs me. I let out a huff.

"Don't trouble yourself. I'll tend to all this later," I tell her, still looking out the window at the girls in the pool. Brilliant sun glistens off Abbie's sunscreen-slick body. I swallow hard and try to focus on Jude's play in the water.

"It's no trouble at all, Mr. Ratliff," Esmeralda says, ever the loyal subject in my rapidly decaying kingdom.

"Please. It isn't for you to fret over. It was a childish move on my part, one that my ex-wife would partake in, and isn't becoming. I'll handle the cleaning. Think of it as my penance."

I finally look over my shoulder at her and force a smile.

"As you wish." Light humor laces her voice. She's

trying to cheer me up, referencing a movie we once watched together in the early days, before Natasha and Abbie and even little Jude entered my life.

Esmeralda has been at my side a long time. Loyal as ever. *When,* I wonder, *will she also betray me?*

"I'm terribly busy at the moment, so if you just came to check on me..."

She nods. "Understood, sir. However, Mr. Montgomery is here. He's asked to see you."

Perfect. Just perfect. The last fucking thing I need right now.

I set the tumbler down on my desk and nod. "Ah. I was wondering when he'd arrive."

"Shall I send him in, or...?" she asks hesitantly.

I rub my hands over my face and lean back in my chair, my throne, behind the massive wooden desk. "His daughter is in the pool with Jude. You may send him there to retrieve her."

Esmeralda clears her throat. "He wishes to speak to you. Directly."

"I do not wish to speak to him. Tell him I am unavailable."

"I already did, sir, but. Well. You know how he is."

My jaw clenches. I know very well the kind of man Ford Montgomery is. He, like me, seldom takes no for an answer and fulfills his desires without recourse. Which is how I know he won't leave my estate without seeing me, nor will he leave without an answer as to why I won't see my oldest friend. Despite the fact that we've drifted apart in the past several years, I'd still hoped to avoid looking into the eyes of this man. The man I've betrayed by deflowering his daughter.

Shaking my head, I wave a hand impatiently. "Very well. Send him in."

Esmeralda nods and exits the room, leaving the door open. Her sensible heels click across the hallway's marble floors and are soon joined by a heavier set of steps, reverberating down my spine like a priest's bell at confession.

The sour feeling in my gut threatens to overtake me as soon as Ford enters my office, hands in his pockets like it's a day at the damn boardwalk. He pauses in the doorway, surveying the mess instead of greeting me. This breathes anger into my lungs. These things are not for his eyes. I should have had Esmeralda clean up. I should have never lost control to begin with.

"Busy morning?" he finally asks.

I deflect my lingering guilt by letting my fury come to a full boil.

"I see you've finally come to escort your daughter home," I respond coldly.

"Hm. I think you and I need to have a chat, old friend." He doesn't move from the doorway. "May I sit, or should we conduct this in a room with fewer sharp objects?"

"There was a hornet. Things got messy trying to kill it." I keep my voice smooth and level, though he knows me well enough to easily see through the lie. Still, he doesn't remark upon it. "We could have easily spoken over the phone, you know."

"We've been friends a decade and a half and you'd relegate me to a phone call?" Ford says. He crosses the room to my bar, lifting the decanter of bourbon and pouring himself a glass, then gesturing toward my empty one. "Do you need a refill?"

"You have no business waltzing into my home after what happened." Though I am thoroughly ruffled at the sight of another Montgomery pawing through my belongings, I keep myself stoic, affecting a stiff upper lip. "As I'm sure you are aware."

"Is that right?" He takes a drink and nods appreciatively, then brings the bottle over to my desk to refill my glass. I cover it with my hand, but he brushes me away and pours two fingers worth. "I have to admit, Graham, I'm frankly a bit puzzled by your actions."

"*My* actions?" I scoff. "Of anyone here, my actions are not the ones under investigation."

Ford glances at the tabloids littering my desk. "I think we both know that isn't the case."

"Don't patronize me."

"Friends don't patronize. They tell the truth." He sits in the chair across from me and comfortably crosses one leg over the other. "You told me that years ago."

I shake my head. "I was full of shit then."

"Still are." Ford smiles and takes another drink. "This is damn good. Woodford?"

This charade sets my teeth on edge. "Collect your daughter and go, if you please. We have nothing to discuss."

"I beg to differ. You see, this situation indirectly involves me and our previous arrangement." He takes another drink, his eyes never leaving mine. "This is all about optics, old friend."

"You don't know what's happening in my house."

He raises a brow. "*You* don't know what's happening in your house. Abbie didn't sell your story."

"You don't know that," I scoff.

It's his turn to scoff. "Bastard. You should know better than to insult me and my kin."

"You'll forgive me if I'm not overflowing with generosity at present. But does it even matter whether she did or didn't?" I gesture to the tabloids spread out on the desk. "The story is out there, regardless. And I cannot have this image."

"The image where you fuck my daughter and then fire her is not better."

Heat floods through me.

"I'm not fucking her," I state, ignoring the fact that I'm once again telling a bald-faced lie to someone I know I can't get away with lying to.

"Then there's no reason to fire her," Ford says sensibly. He leans forward. "Look. We both know these magazines are a load of horse manure. Are you telling me you believe Abbie went behind your back and hired someone to follow you around town and take unflattering photos, and then sold some cockamamie story for a quick buck? All while she's busy taking what seems like damn good care of the daughter you aren't particularly inclined to spend time with?"

"Ford," I warn dangerously.

He shrugs, his nonchalance only serving to stoke my rage all the more.

"Tell me I'm wrong." He sets his glass down on my desk and spreads his hands. "Right now. Tell me I'm wrong and I'll walk out that door and take my daughter with me."

We hold eye contact for a minute too long and I regret that I'm the first to break it. "I'm under an incredible amount of stress right now. Natasha's having a field day over this. She's threatening to take me to court for full custody. She's trying to eat my head for breakfast."

"The praying mantis always eats her suitors, Graham. And how do you know this isn't her doing? It wouldn't be beneath her."

"Natasha would never," I say. But I don't know if I believe that. In fact, the more I think about it, the more I have to consider that Natasha is exactly the person behind this.

"So you believe your ex-wife over my daughter?" He stares me down again.

"I—no. I don't know."

Everything about this feels wrong. The worst of it, the whole bastard of it, is I can't seem to find the up and down in this scenario. I don't know what or whom to believe.

"You need to *fix this*," Ford says. His voice is steel. I see a familiar fire in his eyes that I haven't seen in a long time. "It's not just your image at stake here. If you think you can just smear my daughter's reputation, give her the boot and destroy her life, then you've forgotten exactly what I can do when I'm displeased."

An old memory shakes loose, one where Ford ruined a man who crossed him. It wasn't just about pride or petty revenge, either—he bankrupted the man, got him blacklisted in his own industry, then sent the IRS after the man's brother-in-law's tractor business as well, which subsequently folded. Everything the man had worked to build over the course of two decades was torched to the ground after he tried to double-cross Ford in a business deal.

Ford Montgomery is brutal. I've always sworn to stay out of his warpath, and yet I've found myself impossibly, squarely in the middle of it.

"What do you expect me to do?" I finally ask through gritted teeth.

"I don't know and I don't give a shit. It's your mess to figure out, old friend." The grim set to his features is replaced once again with that breezy affability. "But you will take care of my daughter, and you will ensure this shitshow ends. Cheers."

He clinks his glass with mine, still left unattended on the desk, and drains the last of the bourbon. Then he stands and gives me a nonchalant salute, as though we were just sitting here discussing golf tournaments. He straightens his cuffs and leaves without another word, his footsteps echoing down the hall once again.

I turn to watch the girls in the pool again, where Ford stops to talk to his daughter. They exchange a few words, where he points directly to my office window, and then he kisses her on the top of the head. And leaves. Without taking her.

My blood is suddenly boiling. My best friend just came in here and strong-armed me, I have no idea what to believe about who planted this fucking story, and now I'm stuck with a very serious problem living under my roof.

Said problem adjusts her bikini, untying and retying the halter around her neck, and for just a moment, I think she's going to take the top off entirely. Then she adjusts her cleavage one final time and dives straight down into the clear blue water of the pool, Jude's shrieks of joy reaching all the way up here.

I'm not keeping Abbie. I'm not. I'll have to find a way to get rid of her.

Even if I really do want to fuck all my frustration right out with her.

Chapter Four

Abbie

It amazes me sometimes how kids can sense that things are off at home, especially Jude. She's a smart little thing who seems to easily pick up on the oscillating moods of her father, withdrawing into herself every time he's in a mood. I always have to work extra hard to pull her out of it. But right now, I could use a bit of cheering up myself.

I don't know what the official status is of my employment in the house, only that my dad said he fixed everything. But Graham still hasn't spoken to me since he threw all those tabloids at me in his office. Am I still employed here? Probably. Will Graham ever talk to me again? That's going to take some extra work.

Like Amanda said, though, I just need to find a way to prove Natasha did it so I can clear my name and win back Graham's trust. From what I've seen and heard of his ex-wife, it isn't beyond her to do something this crass and awful. Poor Jude, having a mother like that. Mine may have her flaws, but she's always loved and protected me—she'd never use me as a pawn against my father. I can't say the same about Natasha Ratliff.

Jude's lessons are finished for the day, so she and I are in the stables visiting the horses.

"Desi looks really good." I nudge Jude slightly with my elbow and grin big at her. "You do such a great job taking care of her."

"Thanks," Jude says softly. Then she adds, "She really likes being groomed. Sometimes horses can get skittish about it, but Des loves it. Look what she does when I brush her neck."

Jude demonstrates, and I laugh as Desi stretches her neck and whickers softly. I catch a brief smile from Jude, and then she returns her full focus to the horse. She's been quiet all day.

Her silence tugs at my heart. "Do you want to braid some ribbons in her mane? I bet she'd look amazing!"

"Sure," is the only response I get back.

"Did someone say ribbons?" Cassie asks, appearing at the door of Desi's stall. "We just got a bunch of new ones, if you want to come take a look."

"Okay." Jude is flat and monotonous with her one-word answers.

Cassie and I exchange worried glances, and then Jude and I follow Cassie through the stables to the tack room where they keep the riding equipment and other supplies.

"It's been a while since the horses have been properly gussied up," Cassie says. "You want to help me out with that today, Jude?"

Jude shrugs her consent.

I brought her here in the hopes of perking her up, but it's been a hard sell. It's strange—I've never seen Jude so glum around horses. I was sure she'd brighten up immediately.

"What if we gave each pair of them some matching ribbons?" I suggest brightly, overdoing it a little. "Lucy and Desi can have matching colors, and Donnie and Daisy can have another matching set. That'd be so cute."

"Can they be complementary colors?" Jude asks, a little hesitant, as though she's afraid to show too much enthusiasm.

"Of course they can," I tell her, sorting through the drawer of brightly colored ribbons. "What are you thinking? Donald Duck had a blue outfit and Daisy wore pink and purple. Lucy and Desi are trickier because their TV show was in black and white, you know? Maybe we can give them something fun, like a black-and-white checkerboard pattern and a lime green."

Jude screws up her face. "Lime green?"

"Yeah!" I can't help laughing a little at the sour expression on her face. "Or is that a no? Okay, that looks like a no. Apparently I am no good at picking colors."

"There's a pretty apple red around here somewhere," Cassie suggests, coming up with a roll of ribbon that looks so delicious, Snow White would probably eat it without a second thought. "It would look beautiful with Desi's coat."

Jude's eyes light up, just a little. "That's perfect," she coos.

"Do we have any pretty greens?" I ask, poking around

the stash. "Red and green would be a really nice pair for Desi and Lucy."

"It'd be like Christmas!" Jude's fully into it now, elbowing her way into the drawer and pawing through it excitedly. "I love Christmas colors."

"Ooh, genius. Christmas in July is totally a thing," I tell her, smiling at her excitement. "What if we braid in some bells, too?"

"Can't. Desi doesn't like bells." Jude shakes her head, but she looks thoughtful. "Are there any with glitter?"

"You've got a good eye, Jude." Cassie winks at me. "Red and glitter would look stunning in her mane."

"This one!" Jude squeals, holding the ribbon up triumphantly. "And if we have a dark green, she'll look like a Christmas tree!"

"Ooh, and Lucy will look like a holly bush!" I nudge her gently again, and this time Jude nudges me back with a bright grin. "Maybe we can even find some garland or twinkle lights somewhere, and we can decorate their stalls?"

"Christmas in July!" Jude claps her hands excitedly.

Relief floods through me, seeing her finally start to cheer up. I hate to think she's been so down because of me. If she ever sees those trashy magazines, my God. I don't know what she would do, or think, or if she would even understand what it all means.

"We've got a stash of holiday decorations here in the barn," Cassie says. "I can pull them out and we can see what's what."

"Best day ever!" Jude claps and skips back to Desi's

stall, ribbons clutched tightly in her hands. "Come on, Abbie!"

"I'm coming, I'm coming!" I call after her with a laugh. I grab Cassie's arm and lower my voice. "Thank you so much. She's been having a rough time."

Cassie's brows draw together in sympathy. "Does she know about...what happened?"

"No. At least I don't think so. It's just been kinda tense at the house. Graham's been avoiding me like the plague, and it's not like she doesn't notice his attitude changed."

"Poor thing. And you, too. I've been worried ever since I saw the headlines. I just didn't want to overstep or stick my nose where it doesn't belong." Cassie squeezes my hand.

I sigh. "Everyone else who works here knows too, don't they?"

She looks away. "Yeah. I mean, the news is everywhere. It's kind of hard not to know."

My stomach drops. "Jesus. Look, whatever you've seen or read—I didn't do it. I swear."

"I never thought you would."

"Thanks. No one else believes me." I don't have to say exactly who I'm talking about, because I can tell she already knows. "But why would I even do that to him? And why would I ruin everything I have going on here?"

"I know. But it'll all blow over. Just give it some time." She gives me a reassuring smile. "Besides, everyone knows the tabloids are garbage. Only an idiot would really believe them."

I don't say anything, because calling Graham Ratliff

an idiot isn't going to make me feel any better, though I wish it would.

"Anyway, just know I'm in your corner," she adds. "And I'm here if you need to talk."

My chest feels a little lighter. "Thank you. It means a lot. Really."

"Abbie!" Jude calls from Desi's stall.

"Oops. Duty calls." I smile at Cassie.

"Go on. I'll get the box of decorations and bring them over."

When I get to Desi's stall, I find Jude braiding the horse's mane with the ribbons, and Desi standing placidly, chewing on an oatmeal treat.

"Desi is super excited for her ribbons," Jude tells me.

"I'll bet. I don't think anyone takes as good care of their horses as you do."

"They get me," Jude says sagely, finishing a braid. "We understand each other."

"Who understands each other?" a sharp, familiar voice says from the stall door, instantly making my stomach clench.

"Mommy!" Jude shouts, dropping the braid and dashing into her mother's arms.

Natasha stands there dramatically clutching Jude to her chest with an imperious expression on her face, looking like she's posing for a movie still. She's wearing dark slacks, a silk blouse, and more jewelry than I've ever seen all in one place, outside of an actual jewelry store. Every finger is adorned with gemstones and gold. Her hair is pulled back in a sleek French twist. She looks immaculate. And wildly overdressed for the stables.

"That's my sweet girl." She kisses the top of Jude's head and pulls back to smile at her daughter. "What are you up to?"

"Abbie's helping me braid Desi's mane," Jude says with a grin.

"You like hanging out with your new nanny, huh?" Natasha gently cups Jude's cheeks in her hands.

Jude nods. "She's fun!"

"Is she? Well, I'm glad. *Nannies* should be fun."

Natasha doesn't spare me a glance as she talks about me, even though I'm standing mere feet away. I feel like dirt, being reminded that I'm just the nanny—even though it's true.

"She's going to help me braid Lucy's next!" Jude adds.

"That sounds lovely. Tell you what, darling, I need to go talk to your daddy for a minute, but after that I'll come back and help you myself. How does that sound?"

My cheeks grow hot. My hatred for this woman runs so, so deep. Especially knowing she is probably the one who sabotaged my relationship with Graham.

Jude shoots a cautious glance at me, but I smile back at her and nod.

"Okay," Jude says.

"I'll be right back." Natasha kisses her head once more and turns to leave without ever acknowledging me.

Once she's gone, Jude finishes the braid and then we wait around outside Lucy's stall for a few minutes, which soon turns to twenty. "When do you think my mom will be back?"

"I don't know. You want to go to the house and

rustle up a snack while we wait?" I ask, trying to keep my voice cheerful and even. I don't tell her that I'm dying to try to listen in on Natasha's conversation with Graham, even though they're probably sequestered in his office.

"Okay, sure." Jude shrugs and we make our way back to the main house.

We haven't even closed the door behind us when we hear raised voices erupting from the direction of Graham's study. Jude freezes as her parents' angry words hit a crescendo, combining into one massive wall of yelling. It's impossible to make out what they're even saying.

"Hey," I whisper softly, immediately regretting my decision to bring Jude here with me. "Why don't you head back to the stables and I'll bring the snack out to you, okay? I'm sure they're just...trying to work some things out."

Jude hesitates, her large eyes darting worriedly down the hall.

"It'll be okay. Maybe you can see if Cassie found those Christmas decorations yet," I say gently, and nudge her toward the door.

As soon as she's gone, I pad down the hallway toward the study. But before I can get close enough to eavesdrop, the voices go quiet and the door flies open. I quickly duck into a guest bathroom and out of their line of sight, holding my breath as I cower behind the door.

"I think we're done here," I hear Graham say curtly.

"Good. It's settled then," Natasha says, her heels clicking on the hallway floor as she exits Graham's study.

"I'll be moving back in tomorrow. Now I need to go make the arrangements."

My heart freezes, and then I hear what must be the study door closing. All I can do is stand there in shock as Natasha makes her way back through the house and out the door.

I feel like I can't breathe. Natasha is moving back in?

Reality hits me square in the gut. It's over.

Everything Graham and I had is really and truly over.

Chapter Five

Graham

THE DEVIL WALKS into my office wearing a white silk blouse and trousers as black as her soul. All the flashy jewelry with which she adorns herself may as well represent body counts. Bodies she's lusted after, bodies she's attained, bodies she's slayed under her ridiculously long red nails. She smells of expensive perfume and the lingering hay and leather scent of the stables.

Natasha must have visited Jude before coming in here, which means our daughter knows her mother is in the house—which means we only have a short window of time to talk before Jude comes looking for her. Hopefully Abbie can keep her distracted, which is the only current perk of still having the Montgomery girl in my house.

"Hello, Graham," my ex-wife says breezily upon her arrival, and I intuit by both her dress and her demeanor that she's here with some kind of business proposition for me. But I'd rather die than agree to anything she puts on the table.

I suppose it's fortunate that I've already broken everything within her reach.

"I don't believe I called for an exorcism," I say dryly.

"Cute." Natasha smiles tightly. "But by that logic, I'm the priest."

"God himself would rot if that was ever the case."

"You said it, not me." She takes a long, sweeping survey of my office in a manner I don't appreciate, like she's sizing it up for herself. She pointedly avoids looking at me, taking it all in, before settling on the bar cart. "Drink? Perhaps a—"

"This won't take long enough," I cut her off, extending an arm toward a chair instead. "To what do I owe the displeasure?"

"Can we just drop all the pretenses, Graham?" she says sweetly, coming over to the desk and leaning over it. "You know exactly why I'm here."

"As I already told you on the phone, nothing regarding the custody of our child changes without a court order."

She smiles. "I'm sorry to hear you feel that way. However, it's not unexpected. Which is why I'm here with an ultimatum for you." Natasha cups my cheek for a moment, making my skin crawl, and then gives it a light slap. "We're playing by my rules now."

"You have no rules."

"Of course I do." She says it so matter-of-factly, it's infuriating. "I've always had rules; they were just more relaxed than your strait-laced bullshit. But no matter. You've crossed a line, darling. And now I have the upper hand."

"I am not, in fact, sleeping with my nanny, so unfortunately you haven't a leg to stand on in a court of law," I say hotly. The lie is getting easier every time I tell it. I'm almost starting to believe I'm innocent.

"Oh, really?" Natasha shoots back. "That's not what several reliable sources have said."

"You call the tabloids a *reliable source*?"

"More reliable than you." She turns her back to me and sashays over to the bar to pour herself a drink. Then she takes a long sip, relishing it, and says, "Either Jude leaves with me today, or I move back in. Just think, Graham. We can all be one big, happy family again."

I stare at her as she slowly swallows down the rest of the drink, down to the last drop. She licks her lips and lets out a low moan. Then she sets the empty glass down and smiles.

All I can do is stare in horrified disbelief, still in shock at the words that just slithered out of her mouth. What kind of ultimatum is this? She has absolutely no tangible proof to back up her claim that I'm an unfit parent, and yet here she is, threatening me? Absolutely the fuck not.

"How about option three," I say. "You leave my house at once."

"Absolutely. I'll be glad to do that. With Jude." She slinks past me, over to the windows, then turns and crosses her arms as if she once again owns everything under this roof. "You see, Graham, here's the skinny. Everyone thinks you're a lecherous old man who sleeps with the help. The teenaged help. Not only that, but you've put our daughter in danger by entrusting her care to the kind of person who spends more time on her back than with our child."

"That is absolutely not true—"

"And if I leave Jude in this unhealthy environment, I'll be leaving her in harm's way."

I'm so angry, I can't sit still anymore. Rising from my chair, I storm toward her. "Come off it, Natasha! I've already told you the stories are bullshit."

"Isn't that interesting. They were on point when they covered me, but when the attention turns to you, it's all lies?" She goes over to my desk chair and drops into it, giving it a spin.

"Get out." My jaw is clenched and I'm doing my best to keep my shit together, but I don't know how much longer I can hold out.

"As I said, I'm happy to. I'll just get Jude and have her pack a bag so we can go." She doesn't move, but smiles at me with all the warmth of a Great White.

"You will not."

"Wonderful—then I'll move my things in this evening."

"Did you hear me?" My voice booms across the room, losing the battle with control. "Get out of my house!"

"I don't think *you* heard *me*," she yells, her voice rising to meet mine. "You have two choices before I light your ass up with the help of my very expensive, very competent family lawyer. We'll have no trouble putting together a lengthy legal document detailing your absences, your work schedule, your sordid affairs, the danger you've put our child in—"

"She's never been in danger!" I long for something to throw, to terrify her into silence.

"Is that right?" Natasha all but purrs. "Who cared for Jude while you were busy fucking your nanny? That was the word we settled on, wasn't it?"

"You are the adulterer in this house, Natasha. Not me."

"Hm. Well." She stands and walks over to me, oozing evil as she hisses, "I will bring you to your motherfucking knees in a heartbeat, Graham Ratliff. Try me. Try me over something as important as our daughter, and see what happens."

"Fuck you."

"You would be so lucky." She digs a finger into my chest. "You know what the funniest part is? I don't even think you did it, Graham. I was eaten alive by those same piranhas ages ago. I know how the media machine works."

"What are you talking about?" I sputter. "There was photographic evidence, for fuck's sake! You had multiple affairs over the course of our marriage!"

"Hush, now." Natasha presses a finger to my lips. "I'm here to fix your little fuckup, but as I said, we're playing by my rules. I'll be moving my things back in shortly. Are we clear?"

She has me over a barrel and she knows it. I won't lose Jude. I can't lose my daughter.

All I can do is nod in agreement, watching Natasha's face transform into an expression of self-satisfied, hideous triumph as she revels in her victory.

For a moment, I'm so bloody angry that my mind goes

blank. What the hell happened to my life? Just a few days ago, everything was perfect...and now it's like I've fallen down Alice's rabbit hole. The woman who captured my heart sold me out, her father—my oldest friend—threatened me, and now the devil herself is holding my nuts over a fire. And there's nothing I can do about it but let her have the final word. I'm completely, utterly trapped.

"I think we're done here," I manage.

"Good. It's settled then." Natasha glides out of my office, head held as high as her expensive heels, pausing to turn back around and toss off a smug, "I'll be moving back in tomorrow. Now I need to go make the arrangements."

As soon as she's out of sight, I sink back into my chair. "No fucking way."

No way will I let this happen. That serpent is not moving back into my house, nor is she taking my daughter. There has to be a way out. I can't give in to Natasha's blackmail.

I grab my phone and call my lawyer, Elise Bowen. She's a total hard ass, a Yale graduate, and bills at $2,000 per hour. She's also a fan of whiskey. We're old friends.

Elise answers in two rings. "Bowen." Glad to see she honors our arrangement.

I fill her in on what happened while I pour a drink and shoot it down. I pour a second one and take it back to my desk. "Tell me she's full of shit, Bow. I need you to get me out of this."

"It's hard to say which way a judge would rule." Sounds of typing echo over the line. "But unfortunately, she may not be bluffing. Affairs happen all the time, of course, but she lost custody of Jude over hers. The courts might have more to say now that you're embroiled in a scandal yourself—especially one involving the person directly responsible for her care."

"It's a bullshit story. It's in the tabloids, for fuck's sake!"

She's silent for a moment. "The story is everywhere, Graham. It's starting to crop up on more credible news outlets. It's...not looking good. You've got a leak somewhere."

My throat tightens. "I didn't do it."

"I don't give a shit if you did or didn't. You could be fucking that girl twice on Sunday and I wouldn't care, as long as she's over eighteen. But you clearly have someone close to you with loose lips, and the ship's going to sink if you can't figure it out and plug the damn leak."

"How am I supposed to do that?" I all but snarl.

"I have a private investigator who might be able to help, if you're interested."

The idea of someone poking around in my personal business makes the hairs on my neck stand up, but hasn't the worst already happened? "I'm interested. Make the call."

"My assistant already has him on the other line. I'll talk to him. In the meantime, play nice with Natasha. I hate to say it, but you don't want her as an enemy right now. And you don't want her to get suspicious that you're working on mounting a defense behind her back."

"Fine." I sigh. Out in the hallway, I spy Abbie walking by, trying to look innocent. She must have been eavesdropping. "Thanks, Bow. Talk soon."

45

"You got it. Give me a ring next time you're in Manhattan."

I hang up the phone and call Abbie into the study. She steps over the threshold hesitantly, like she wasn't expecting me to see her tiptoeing past my door. This girl, she's absurd. Terrible at flirting, terrible at sneaking around, apparently terrible at keeping her lips sealed about our relationship. Even if she didn't go to the press herself, she had to have blabbed to someone who did. It makes me furious at her all over again. She ruined everything.

"Hi," she murmurs softly, her blue eyes locking on mine. "Did you...want me?"

Heat rushes through me hearing those words, even though she meant them innocently. But I'm still so turned on by her. I can feel the phantom of her mouth around my cock.

No. I can't lose control. That's how I got into this mess. And was it worth it? Fuck no.

"What I want is for you to stop lurking about outside my doors trying to eavesdrop," I tell her coldly. "I assume you heard everything?"

She stares down at her feet, looking like she got hit by a truck. "I heard you're getting back together with Natasha."

I scowl. "It's not your business."

"Not my business?" She looks up at me with those doe eyes, both terrified and angry all at once. "Graham, she's so bad for Jude. You know it's true. What's going to happen when—"

"Maybe you should have thought of that before you told everyone in town about us."

The color drains from her face. "I didn't. And I didn't leak the story."

"Someone did, and it wasn't me. Which leaves you. But it doesn't matter. What's done is done."

I open my laptop and wave her off to let her know the conversation is over.

"You can't do this!" Abbie rushes to my desk. "Please, don't do this. You've seen it yourself. Natasha doesn't care about Jude; she only shows up when she wants something from you. And Jude—God, you've seen the way it upsets her. She always thinks her mom is coming back to spend time with her, only to be abandoned over and over again."

"Enough of your histrionics," I interrupt, smashing my fist on the desk. "I'm not interested in hearing you plead your case. The decision's been made. Now go."

Her chin wobbles, but I refuse to let myself be affected by it. "I didn't leak that story, Graham. You have to believe me." Her voice drops to a harsh whisper. "Why *can't* you believe me?"

"Because you've done nothing but prove you're untrustworthy," I snap. "Time and time again. What happened between us was a mistake, and it's time you recognize that. *It's over, Abbie*. We're done."

"You're breaking my heart!" she wails, hands cupped over her face.

"You broke mine first," I snarl, pushing back from the desk and stalking across the room, past Abbie, down the hall, before I can regret exposing myself like that, before

47

she has a chance to take advantage of my weakness, before I have a chance to see her completely fall apart at the harshness of my words.

It's over. It was over when the news broke, but now it is fully and completely over. My only goal now is recovering from this mess and protecting Jude. There is no room for Abbie in my life.

Not anymore.

Chapter Six

Graham

My ex is maddeningly punctual when she wants to be, and today is no different. Within hours, Natasha's boxes begin arriving at my home as though she's been planning this for weeks.

Maybe she *has* been planning this for weeks. Ford's warning echoes in my ears: *How do you know this isn't her doing?*

"I fucking don't," I mutter to myself, watching another armload of boxes get marched through my front door.

But it doesn't make a difference whether Natasha orchestrated this whole thing or not. Because she's here to stay. At least, she is until my lawyer can dig up something solid that we can use against her.

Outside, it's organized chaos at its finest. Natasha is directing the movers and my entire staff as she stands beside a moving truck, phone in one hand, purse in the other, acting like she's the queen of the castle. Ire radiates through me. This is my staff, my house. Not hers.

Except it *is* hers, because she's got my balls in her fist and can squeeze whenever she feels like it. It appears she's going to feel like it quite often. I swallow down the resentment climbing up my throat. I hate this woman. I hate what she did to this family. I hate what she did to Jude. I hate what she's currently doing to me. And there's no escape.

I leave my hands in my pockets and aim for a leisurely stroll to meet her on the circular drive, ducking under pieces of furniture being hefted by broad men in sweaty blue shirts bearing the name of the moving truck logo on them.

"I see you came prepared." I keep the venom in my voice at bay and try to sound light and airy, nonchalant, like I don't have a care in the world despite this demon waltzing back into my life.

"That's what staff is for, darling."

"Mm. Are you sure you haven't been planning this for a while?" I watch two burly men struggle with a heavy bench that I recognize from its former life in front of our shared marital bed. "Scheming ways to get back into the house once your lovers were finished with you?"

"Please." Natasha waves me off, still directing traffic, as though I am a mere nuisance, a fly buzzing about her ear, instead of the owner of the estate. "Don't come after me with such gross accusations when I'm the one who came to your rescue to graciously save your ass."

"Right, save my ass. This has nothing to do with an ulterior motive."

"The only person who had ulterior motives was you." She gently pats my cheek and scoops up a satchel by her feet. "Now, if you'll excuse me, I've had a very long day of packing and would like to rest. I assume the bedroom hasn't moved locations?"

"Vampires have to be invited in, you know."

"Oh yes, of course, how silly of me." She brushes back a lock of hair and smiles cheerily. "Graham Ratliff, you are hereby invited into my home, the Ratliff Manor."

"Charmed." The word comes out hot like volcanic lava, but it bounces off her smooth exterior and lands in a puddle amongst the boxes and bags being threaded through my house with a needle made of bone. "We need to lay down some ground rules."

"Absolutely." Natasha's smile grows even wider, if that's humanly possible. "I agree. We need to be on the same page. We can talk in the bedroom while I'm getting changed."

"We'll talk in my *office*, where I conduct all my business." I struggle to keep the fire from my mouth.

"Oh, fine. Be that way." She stands and stares at me expectantly, and it's then I realize she's waiting to follow me in. Like a real vampire.

"Why don't you pour yourself a drink, and I'll meet you in there," I tell her once we're in the foyer, gesturing her down the hall and then stepping away to locate my most loyal employee. "Esmeralda!"

"Yes, sir?" her comforting voice sounds behind me a moment later.

"Please have all of the former Mrs. Ratliff's things moved to the largest guest room in the west wing of the house. You know she keeps irregular hours, and I don't want her too close to Jude." Or Abbie, though I don't say it out loud. Natasha will unhinge her jaw and swallow that girl whole if I'm not careful.

"Understood." Esmeralda nods, and if she's gleaned anything juicy about my personal life from what I've just said, she keeps it to herself.

In my office, I find Natasha reclining on the couch, whiskey in one hand, her phone in the other. She looks as much a part of the room as the bar does, and it unsettles me to see it. I don't like having her in here. I don't want her in here. I don't want any of this to be happening.

When I find whoever leaked this story to the press, I'm going to pull a page from Ford's playbook and destroy their entire life in reciprocation for how they destroyed mine.

"Drink?" Natasha draws the word out around her glass. "I left yours on the bar."

"You think me an alcoholic." I pick up the glass and give it a sniff. Familiarity calms me.

"Birds of a feather," she murmurs.

"Speak for yourself."

I swallow a small mouthful and grab a chair from in front of my desk by one hand. I spin it around and settle into it backwards, a move I've practiced hundreds of times in the boardroom, back when I was still the young, hip, cool executive who wanted to hear good news. Natasha remembers the move, because she snorts.

"You may have my nuts in a vice, but this is still my house," I warn her.

"That's such a dour way to look at it."

"Don't patronize me when you're the one who gave

me an ultimatum." I point at her with the glass. "I'm doing this for Jude. Not you."

"Of course." She nods, settling back into the leather. "I'll entertain this. For now. So what are these so-called ground rules of yours?"

She smiles, clearly not believing my decrees will be long-term.

"I'm serious, Natasha. I don't care what you think you can do to me; you aren't the only one in the room with an attorney."

"Mm, and how is Elise doing? Still licking her wounds from that messy divorce? She had a custody battle of her own to contend with, didn't she?"

I hate this woman more than there are stars in the sky. "She runs one of the most successful and well-regarded law firms in the entirety of the United Kingdom and the States. She's doing just fine."

"Good." She nods, eyebrows raised, mouth cocked in a half-smile. "Do go on."

"Rule number one." I clear my throat, hoping this won't drag out any longer than necessary, lest things get as nasty as they have in the past. "You do not sleep in my room."

Natasha raises a brow. "Come now, what will Jude think? That won't work."

"Jude doesn't go in my bedroom." I savor the sting of the whiskey going down my throat. "And it doesn't matter anyway. We'll tell her you're staying with us for a while, but she is not to think we're reconciling. To be clear, we aren't getting back together. You're just in the house."

"Well, that's ridiculous. She's eight years old, Graham. She's going to have questions."

"And she'll get the answers I deem appropriate. Nothing more, nothing less." I stare down Natasha with firm glare. "To reiterate. You are not to stay in my room. You are not to act as if we are romantically inclined, because I do not love you. You are not to—"

"Now wait one tiny little minute," she interrupts with a voice that threatens, despite its cheery tone. "The whole point of me moving back in—"

"Was to be with Jude, correct?" I give her another hard stare. "You wanted to be near our daughter, and out of the goodness of my heart, I took you back in."

"That's a curious way to say 'nuts in a vice,' don't you think?"

"I could have easily fought you on this in a long, drawn-out court battle, and you know it. We're doing this for the benefit of our child."

"Fine. No hanky-panky and no telling Jude that Mommy and Daddy are together forever," Natasha says around the rim of her glass. She looks expectantly at me. "What else?"

"This is still my home. These are my staff. You do not run this place like it is yours. You will be respectful to my staff at all times."

"Graham, I'm appalled. You act like I don't know how to behave."

"You don't. I lost a lot of good people due to your... indiscretions. I will not have the same thing happen again. Understood?"

"Perfectly." She bats her eyes at me. "I'm very good when I need to be. What else?"

"That's it. We're done here. You'll be in the blue guest room in the west wing."

"Very well." She nods agreeably. "This is your home, these are your rules, and I am grateful for the opportunity to see my darling Judey more often. But just one thing?"

"Go ahead." I blink at her, waiting for the bomb to drop.

"The nanny stays."

"Negative. She's the reason we're here to begin with."

"No, you're the reason we're here to begin with. She's young and a nobody; you are a famous philanthropic businessman with ties everywhere. She stays."

"Impossible," I mutter.

"What's impossible is us parenting," Natasha says. "Look at us, Graham. We both work all the time; we both have personal and professional lives we need to attend to. Playing pat-a-cake has never been our style. And she's wonderful with Jude—surely you've noticed? Or were you too busy checking her out to pay attention to how devoted our Judey is to her?"

I'm fuming but I can't say anything, because yet again, Natasha is infuriatingly correct. Abbie is brilliant with Jude, in ways neither of us could ever hope to be. I've hired numerous nannies over the years and none of them have come close to the way Abbie connects with Jude.

"Besides." She curls up comfortably on the couch, letting her flats drop to the floor. "It will show the whole world how ridiculous that nasty little rumor was. Your *wife* knows you're innocent, and the nanny stays put. That speaks a hell of a lot louder than firing her would."

I sigh, feeling resignation flow through me. I can't refute anything she's said any more than I could when Ford said it. They are good points. Not only that, but keeping Abbie here will ensure that Ford stays off my ass and out of my business and personal affairs. I'd like to think we're better friends than that, that he wouldn't contribute further to the implosion of my life, but this is his daughter we're talking about. I also have a daughter. I know the lengths I would go to in order to protect her.

Pouring myself more whiskey, I take a deep breath. "Fine, then. We'll keep the nanny."

Natasha smiles and it's beautiful, because everything about her is beautiful, because the devil is a well-dressed actress. If nothing else, my ex has just demonstrated exactly how seductive she can be. Even when it isn't about sex, she's a master at getting people to play right into the palm of her hand.

"I knew you'd understand, darling," she says. "And it won't be so bad. It'll be an adjustment, obviously, but trust me—this is the right move. For all parties involved."

It won't be the right move for Abbie, not after her breakdown in my office today. But at some point, I'll have to tell her what Natasha's decided. I'm dreading it.

Because my self-control has failed me around Abbie time and time again. And in the deepest, darkest parts of my mind, I can't hide the dirty thought that I wouldn't mind fucking her one more time.

Chapter Seven

Abbie

Not knowing where I'm laying my head to sleep each night has me in a constant state of anxiety and frustration. My father believes my position is safe, but he didn't see the hatred I did in Graham's eyes. My suitcases have been packed for several days, ready to accompany me far, far away from this nightmare castle, but I have no idea where to go.

Amanda and Cassie have both offered me a place to crash, and I know I can go back home to my parents' house in Connecticut, but nowhere feels like it's the right choice. I can't shake the conviction that I belong here.

Meanwhile, there's been no progress at the Ratliff estate on any front. Graham won't look at me, Jude is perpetually forlorn, and Esmeralda is having a fucking field day shooting me disapproving glances and watching me mope around almost as much as Jude.

I don't know what I did to the housekeeper to have earned her scorn, but even still I'm having doubts that she's the one who ratted me out. Who's the more likely culprit—the gossipy housekeeper or the shunned ex-wife? It's impossible to tell and I don't know how to get to the bottom of it. No one is talking to me and I don't even know how long I'll be here.

It fucking sucks.

A firm knock sounds at my door, and it catches me so off guard I practically jump out of my skin. Only one person knocks as firmly as that in this house. Instantly, my heart careens against my rib cage, desperate and inconsolable. Graham. He hasn't spoken to me since he told me I broke his heart.

Those words are forever cemented into my brain. I've tried to analyze them one hundred different ways and each time it comes back to the same awful conclusion: I had his heart and now it's gone forever. Things were perfect until someone sold our story to the wolves. He never told me he truly cared for me, even though I could have sworn I felt it in my gut, and now it's too late to revel in it. I'm drowning in this heavy sense of irreconcilable loss.

But here he is, now, outside my door.

I crawl across my bed and scamper over to the door, smoothing my hair down as I go. I probably look like crap, but I can't keep him waiting just so I can primp. Whatever he has to say to me, I have to be ready for it. Anything is better than the agony of the purgatory I've been in.

When I open the door, he's standing a step back from me, hands in his pockets, sleeves rolled up, hair a bit disheveled as if he's been running his hands through it.

He looks so good that I feel a little melty, my knees loose and my heart a thundering freight train as I cling to the doorknob for support.

"There's been a development," Graham says, instead of "hello" like a normal person.

"Okay." It's all I can say, because I have no idea what's about to come out of his mouth, and I'm terrified.

"Your services..." Graham trails off, not looking at me.

I am a caged bird, desperate for flight. "Yes?"

He sighs. "We have decided to maintain your services here, as Jude's nanny."

Wait—I'm officially unfired? Relief floods through me, but hearing the decision doesn't fully banish my anxiety. "We?" I repeat.

"You're not keeping this job because of me."

I recoil as if he struck me. His voice is so devoid of emotion, so stony cold, like a damn icicle that impales my soul. Not because of him? Meaning, he wanted me gone. Because he doesn't trust me. Because he doesn't love me. Because he doesn't even like me.

But I *am* keeping this job. Which means not everything is lost. I still have time to prove my innocence and win Graham back. I have a chance to fix this. To do everything in my power to get Graham back. Jude must have begged him to keep me on. She had to be the one who—

"You can thank Natasha." He pushes himself off the wall and heads toward the staircase. "It was one of her terms for moving back in."

"She...wants to keep me?" I ask, not able to keep the surprise from my voice. I thought she hated me. Every time Natasha is around, she seems to go out of her way to make sure I'm aware that I don't belong here, that I'm not good enough. Why would she want to keep me?

"Glad your ears still work," Graham says over his shoulder, stomping down the stairs as if he can't get away fast enough.

Hurt rips through me like a fresh wound. He can't even stomach being around me. How am I supposed to fix this when the mere sight of me elicits such a strong reaction? This is going to be utterly impossible. But I close my eyes and take a deep breath. I'm staying. That's something. I go back into my room and collapse on the bed.

Grabbing my phone, I dial my dad's number, eager to relay the first piece of good news I've gotten in days.

"Calling with an update, I hope?" he answers. "Or do I have to make another long drive up to New York?" His voice is gruff, but not cruel, which I appreciate. I don't think I can take any more scolding today, or anytime soon.

"No. I have good news."

"Spit it out, then."

That riles me up. "Spit it out? Seriously? Things here have been hell and you don't even care."

"They've been hell because you were careless. This is what's known as consequences."

I sigh. "I'm just calling to let you know that I'm officially unfired."

"Good. I told you I'd fix it."

"Actually...Graham said it was because of Natasha." Even saying her name sends a chill down my spine. "He says it was part of her terms for moving back in. Which...I guess is supposed to put a Band-Aid on this whole tabloid thing."

"Interesting." He stresses the word a bit and lets out a low whistle. "Well, this is your second chance. Better not fuck it up."

"I won't." At least, I hope I won't.

"Go get 'em, tiger. And report back soon. I'll be keeping better tabs this time."

"Sure thing, Dad."

He hangs up before I can say anything else. The pitter-pattering in my chest slowly begins to die. I can clear my name, maybe, sure. But doesn't my dad understand the real problem now—there's no way I can possibly get Graham back when his ex-wife is in his bed. And even if she wasn't, he'll barely look me in the face or even talk to me; not exactly conducive to setting up an affair. And I don't want to be "the other woman." I want to be *the* woman. Natasha doesn't belong in his bed. I do.

I need help. I text my best friend, even though I'm not sure Amanda will have any answers, either. She might be way more experienced than me when it comes to guys, but this situation is beyond even her. Talking to her always makes me feel better, though.

She doesn't respond—she's probably out having actual fun during her summer break, unlike some of us—so I end up sending her a mass of text messages, one after the other, unloading all my thoughts and feelings. I know she'll get back to me later with all her usual love and support, but right now, I feel completely alone.

I tell her how devastating this all is. How losing

Graham is the worst thing ever, how I feel like I'm sixteen all over again. Forced to watch him and Natasha be the perfect couple, while my heart aches with wanting him and not being able to do anything about it. Except that it's even worse this time around—because it's not just some crush anymore. I love him for real. I know what it's like to actually *be* with him. And I've lost him. Utterly and completely.

It's not just that I can't have him because he's taken or I'm underage, either, it's that he doesn't want me anymore. He despises me.

I had a taste of the forbidden fruit and then it was ripped away.

Just then, a timid knock sounds on my door. I look up from the pathetic, lovelorn texts on my phone, pulse suddenly kicking. Who would come knocking this soon after Graham, and so quietly? For half a second, I worry it's Natasha and fear seeps into me. What could she possibly have to say? Did she come to threaten me to stay away from Graham?

But when I pull the door open, I find a nightgown-clad Jude staring up at me.

"Hi," she says, looking a little forlorn. "Can I come in?"

"Of course." I usher her in, relieved it's my tiny bestie and not her mother, ready to eat my face. "What's going on?"

Jude settles into the chair in front of the vanity, absently touching all the makeup strewn across the top. Her voice is small as she says, "I just...needed to not be down there."

"Down where?"

She points at the floor, gesturing at what I'm assuming is the first floor, where her parents' voices are swelling around another argument. She sighs. "They fight all the time. It's just like before my mom left. Except worse."

"That must be really hard to listen to." I sit cross-legged on the end of my bed, facing her. "My parents fight a lot, too. I never like hearing it."

"I don't understand why she came back if they're still mad at each other." Jude drags a finger across the desk before picking up a tube of lipstick and turning it over in her hands. "They're not happy together. They think I don't get it, but I'm not stupid."

"Anyone who thinks you're stupid severely underestimates you." I reach over and poke at her knee. "You're one of the smartest people I know, adults included."

Jude beams, but her face quickly falls. "Do you think they're fighting because of me?"

"Oh, honey. Why would they fight because of you?"

"I don't know. My mom said they never fought like this before I came along."

"What? She told you that?" I can't keep the disgust from my voice. What kind of person says something like that to their own kid? No wonder Graham calls Natasha the devil.

"I asked her if they always fought so much. And she said they didn't used to, when they first met. And they didn't have so many responsibilities. Like me." Tears spill out of her eyes. "How do I get them to stop?"

"That is not a job for little girls like you." I try to push as much warmth into my voice as I can. "You're the kid, they are the parents, and they are supposed to be the grown-ups."

"Grown-ups are stupid."

"Oh, yeah. Definitely stupid." I nod eagerly, making her laugh a little.

For the first time, I realize that someone besides me is coping just as poorly to Natasha moving back in—and that's Jude. I had assumed she'd be thrilled to have her mom back, but I obviously didn't consider the fact that Natasha and Graham living under one roof again might be just as traumatic for Jude as having her parents separated. If not worse.

"Do you want to play a game or something?" I shake off the thoughts crowding my mind and try to focus on Jude. "We can finish braiding every mane of every horse in the stables?"

"Even my dad's horses?" She perks up a little.

I laugh. "Every. Single. One. With glitter ribbons."

"And pink!"

"Pink glittery ribbons. Hundreds of them. We can finish decorating for Christmas in July and put jingle bells up everywhere. What do you think?"

Jude chews on her lower lip, but nods. "That sounds fun. Is it too late, though?"

Checking the clock on my nightstand, I shake my head. "Nope. You have a full two hours before it's officially your bedtime. And anything we don't finish, we can pick up again tomorrow. Come on, let's go get our boots on. I'll text Cassie and see if she wants to join us."

I stand to gather her up and head downstairs, ready to distract the both of us from the heartache in the house.

"Thanks, Abbie." Jude grabs my hand. "You're the best friend I've got."

"And you're mine," I tell her.

My heart aches for her. For both of us.

Chapter Eight

Abbie

JUDE and I are in the throes of bringing Christmas early to the stables when she decides we need proper refreshments. I suggest we make a big batch of sugar cookies in the shapes of horses and candy canes, primed for decorating, but she seems less interested in baking and more into testing her braiding skills on every head, mane, and tail in the stables. Myself included.

"Tell you what, then." I flick my ribboned braid over my shoulder and model it while Jude claps and giggles. "I'll go back to the house and see if I can get Mary to bake us some cookies and then we can decorate them tomorrow. Decorating is the fun part."

"Eating them is the fun part!" Jude points out, rummaging around for another glittery ribbon. "Everything else is in the way."

"In the way?" I repeat, laughing at how opinionated she always is. "But you get to savor them better knowing you made them extra special!"

"I savor everything and I'm barely even allowed in the kitchen." She looks and sounds so sage sometimes, it's a total trip. "But if you want to decorate them tomorrow, I'm in. Just make sure we have enough fresh ones to share for now. And milk!"

"Deal." I hold out a pinkie and Jude links it. "I can't wait to frost some pony cookies with you. We can wear scarves and make hot cocoa!"

"It's too hot out for scarves and hot cocoa." She wrinkles her nose.

"Not if we crank down the air conditioning to *negative zero*." I give her shoulder a light squeeze as she starts assessing Cassie's hair. "Will you two be okay for a few?" I ask Cassie.

"Go." She waves me off. "It's my turn in the beauty chair."

I discreetly point at Jude and mouth a *thank you* at Cassie before heading back to the house. Jude's lucky to have Cassie as a riding instructor, and I'm lucky to count her as a friend.

But when I get to the kitchen, it turns out, much to my dismay, that it's Mary's day off. Which means Esmeralda is in charge of all things meal- and snack-related. She's the last person I wanted to see, given that she may or may not have sold me out to the tabloids for money or pure spite or fuck knows what else. Revenge? I honestly haven't figured out a solid motive yet.

"Christmas cookies? In July?" Esmeralda doesn't blink as she ties on an apron and digs around in the pantry looking for holiday-appropriate cookie cutters, but her voice drips skepticism. "Sugar cookies are simple enough, but why do you need all the shapes?"

"We're celebrating Christmas early." I shrug and try to give her my best "I'm just doing my job" look. "Jude needs some cheering up."

"Well. Can't blame her for that." Esmeralda turns on the oven and starts bustling around the kitchen. "Can you get the butter out? I need two sticks."

I pause. This is not my job. And Esmeralda doesn't even like me. I should be getting back to Jude in the stables.

However.

I also know how much Esmeralda likes to gossip, and I could go for a juicy story or two. Maybe this is how my reconnaissance begins.

The kitchen houses a massive commercial refrigerator, easily the size of two regular ones, surrounded by banks of dark wood cabinets. When I open it, I find it crammed with organic produce, twenty-dollar mason jars of turmeric "detox" soup from some bougie grocery store, and various non-dairy milks. It used to be full of juice boxes and Lunchables and applesauce cups and string cheese for Jude's afternoon snacks, but I can't find anything like that now.

"Mrs. Ratliff came in here and threw a fit about the state of the refrigerator," Esmeralda says in a hushed tone over my shoulder, walking past me with two massive sheet pans. "She acts like Mary doesn't know how to feed the family, or like she hasn't been doing it for years, even when Mrs. Ratliff was still here."

"I love Mary's cooking." I finally unearth real butter in the back, buried under a pound of kale and ten different kinds of cloudy, neon-colored bottled juices. "What's wrong with it?"

"You know how actors are." She sniffs and pushes her way into the walk-in pantry, still talking. "What is a juice cleanse, anyway? What exactly is she trying to clean, hmm?"

I'm more than a little thrown off, because she's talking to me like we're old friends, even though she's been snide to me ever since the headlines about me and Graham hit the media. Does she think I'm innocent now? Or am I just the lesser of two evils now that Natasha is back?

"I think it's where you only drink juice for like a week or something," I say.

"No food?" Esmeralda clicks her tongue, setting a bag of flour and a bag of sugar on the island next to the baking powder, baking soda, and vanilla extract. "I guess actors think being skinny is the only way to make a living."

I shrug. "I think it's hard to get consistent work if you don't meet unrealistic beauty standards. Which...I kind of feel sorry for her. That type of pressure can't be fun."

Esmeralda just harrumphs in response. As she rifles through the drawers pulling out measuring cups, spoons, and mixing bowls, I survey the ingredients on the counter, making a mental checklist in my head. My mom and I bake tons of cookies every year for the holidays, so I know a thing or two about the recipes. I only see one thing missing. "Eggs? I didn't see them in the fridge."

"They're over there."

She nods with her chin to an alcove behind the pantry. I go in and find another set of cabinets in a butler's pantry, filled with fresh eggs, various breads, and herbs from the garden.

"This is new," I comment, grabbing the eggs and rejoining Esmeralda at the island.

"Mm. Well, Mrs. Ratliff can only eat farm fresh, cage-free, certified organic eggs, and they cannot possibly be stored in the refrigerator." Esmeralda rolls her eyes heavily and starts to work, combining the ingredients without a recipe. She mumbles irritably under her breath as flour flies through the air.

You know what? I think I like Esmeralda. Maybe she wasn't the one who ratted me out, after all. Maybe she was just protecting her boss and thought that I was trying to put one over on him. Graham said she's been working here for years, which means she must be very loyal. And she clearly dislikes Natasha as much as I do, which makes her an excellent ally.

"Is this a family recipe?" I ask, leaning against the island to watch. "You know it by heart."

"You've got smart eyes." She taps her nose, dusting it lightly with flour. "Mary and I have been working on this recipe for a long time. Mr. Ratliff likes sugar cookies. Not sure he's allowed to have them now, but..." Her voice trails off as she finishes mixing the dry ingredients.

"Surely Na—Mrs. Ratliff can't say no to something that makes Jude so happy?"

Esmeralda snorts. "She can say no to a lot of things. But Mr. Ratliff still runs the house."

"I don't know. He didn't seem to want her here at all, but now she's...back."

"Things are complicated." She looks at me with a very knowing stare.

"I didn't do it," I blurt. "I swear on my grandmother's grave, I didn't say anything to anyone. I wouldn't do that. Especially not for money. I genuinely care about this family."

"Hmph." Esmeralda grunts, but she doesn't argue with me. "Go get the cooling racks from the pantry."

Obediently, I go grab what she asked for and line them up on the counter for when the cookies come out of the oven. "I don't know why no one believes me," I add.

"Because a scorned lover bent on revenge would be the first person to run to the press." She says it without any heat, but more matter-of-fact. "Whether their story is true or not."

"Who says I'm a scorned lover?" I ask, but it comes out a little weak.

Esmeralda raises a brow. "If the shoe fits. But I'm not here to judge."

"Look, regardless, I didn't run to the press—"

"I believe you," she interrupts. "At least, about the tabloid leak."

A huge weight suddenly lifts from my shoulders. "Thanks."

Esmeralda casts a glance over her shoulder before dropping her voice and continuing. "Unfortunately, the result of this mess is that we've been forced to welcome the former Mrs. Ratliff back to the estate. Which isn't making anybody happy. Except Mrs. Ratliff, I suppose."

"I'm sorry," I say. "I know she can be...challenging. To be around."

I slide the bowl of dry ingredients over to her and she begins adding it into the mixing bowl of wet ingredients, letting out a sigh as the cookie dough starts to come together.

"She's always caused problems in the house," Esmeralda says, shaking her head. "She doesn't treat the staff with dignity or respect, like we're her slaves or something."

"I've noticed," I say bitterly.

"And poor Mr. Ratliff," she goes on. "Having to deal with that soul-sucker. He's miserable with her here, too."

My brow furrows. "Aren't they...trying to reconcile? Wasn't that the whole point of having her move back in?"

Esmeralda snorts. "It's just for looks. They're not even staying in the same wing of the house, and even then, she's probably too close for comfort as far as he's concerned. I wouldn't be surprised if he put a deadbolt on his bedroom door to keep her out."

She lets out a little giggle and I force myself to join in, but inside my heart is thumping hard. They aren't sleeping together? They aren't sharing a bed?

There's hope for me yet. I could kiss Esmeralda right on her big mouth. Instead, I watch her roll out the dough, then help press the cookie cutters into it, carefully laying out the candy canes, trees, stars, and oh-so-delicate horse shapes on the baking sheets afterward. When we finish, just over four dozen cookies go into the oven. Plenty to eat and decorate.

Esmeralda dusts her flour-covered hands on her

apron and finally thanks me for my help. "You should get back to Jude, now. These should be done and ready to eat in about twenty minutes or so. I'll bring a batch over to the stables with some milk."

"You sure? Cassie's helping her braid the horses' manes right now, so I can stay here until then. It's no trouble."

She sizes me up for a long moment and then nods firmly. "You're a good girl, Abbie. Just a little liberal with the outfits sometimes. But all the staff like you. You're one of us—part of the family, too."

I can't help but smile. "Thanks, Esmeralda."

"As for tomorrow, I'll gather up all the sprinkles and frosting and food coloring and set them aside in the pantry for whenever our favorite little Ratliff decides she's ready to decorate."

"Thank you so much." I make sure to gush a little, let her feel the appreciation in my voice and tone. "You're the best."

On my way back to the stables, my phone vibrates. It's Amanda, finally texting me back from earlier. My heart soars. I need her insight, and coupled with the new information gleaned from Esmeralda, I feel like I can finally make some progress on my mission to get Graham back.

GET. THAT. MAN., she sends. *Don't let that cheater get her claws back in him.*

I'm not going to be the Other Woman. It's not a good look ☹. I linger outside the stables while I text, close enough to hear Cassie and Jude giggling together, just out of sight.

They aren't sleeping together! They're not even in the same room, she writes back.

Yeah but everyone thinks she's still his wife. That's the whole point. The last thing I need is for the tabloid stories to actually get worse, I type.

Srsly, Abbie?! You aren't breaking up a marriage if they aren't REALLY reconciled. She freaking set you up and now she's trying to make her move to get him back. Stop that bitch.

I text back, *HOW? She's Natasha Ratliff. I'm just... me. You know, the person Graham hates?*

YOU GOTTA GET HIM BACK FIRST!, Amanda shoots back. It makes me wonder just how fast her thumbs are flying. *Slut it up! Get his attention. I know you know how. Wink wink.*

My cheeks burn, because she's right, I do. It just feels different with Natasha here watching my every move out of the corner of her eye. My phone buzzes again.

Didn't he get crazy jealous after your date with that stable boy? Make him jelly again! Get on a hook-up app and talk about it. Loudly.

This makes me laugh. And think. *He did go sorta ballistic after the Quinn thing. Well, and that night with the rando hot guy I met at the bar.*

See? Brag about the number of guys who are into you. You're totes hot, you'll have like a million DMs. You can even get the kid to help you swipe. It'll drive him bonkers.

Shaking my head, I type back, *My God, you're an evil genius.*

Amanda texts back a gif of a cartoon woman in a sexy devil suit.

This is brilliant. This is why I need my friends, and not my jerk-ass dad, to give me advice about Graham. I knew Amanda would be able to help. For the first time in days, I finally feel confident enough to face this mess head-on.

Graham Ratliff will be mine again.

Chapter Nine

Graham

My home is overrun with intruders—bite-y women who think they can undermine me. One issues demands in my own domain and treats my staff like peasants, the other languishes around, drawing in all the lifeforce around her like a succubus. The first is a malicious beast with a dual-pronged tongue who shattered my world, and the second is sex on legs who destroyed everything that was left afterward.

It's no small wonder my whiskey usage has soared. In my bedroom, the sole location where no one can reach me, the bar cart has run clean out. I try to pour one more drink and all that escapes from the bottle, much like the hope I have left, are a few dismal drops.

Donning my robe and muttering obscenities the whole way, I storm to my office for another bottle. Even there it is dire straits, as though someone beat me to it. A thirsty someone who recently moved back in. The same goes for my study, damn her. Which means there is only one place left for me to nick some liquor before bed at this late hour: the kitchen. Mary keeps a secret stash there just for me, which is a necessity when my ex-wife is around.

I pad down the hall, the quiet echoes of my steps promising no other movement within the house. It'll just be me, my whiskey, and silence. Prost.

Just as I get to the kitchen, though, all my hopes are dashed. The freezer door is open, its light cutting through the shadows and shedding unnatural brightness across the floor. I wince. Dealing with Natasha all day is taxing enough. Why should I be forced to grapple with the devil after the sun's gone down, as well? It's tempting to sneak back to my room, avoid the altercation altogether, but I've a wicked headache and the only cure to be found is in here. Bollocks.

Imagine my surprise when I get closer and realize I'm seeing the long, tanned, smooth legs of my nanny instead of my former spouse. She doesn't notice me in the dark, too busy rummaging for ice, so I take the opportunity to drink her in, free and safe from the prying eyes of Natasha and the paparazzi and all the other nosy fucks who can't leave well enough alone.

She's wearing a light, silky, all but see-through camisole and short-shorts set, trimmed in lace, scandalous in any setting, with her hair in long curls. The sight is enough to bring my cock to attention, the bastard, as though she hasn't caused enough destruction already.

There's still a very likely chance she didn't do it, the hungry part of my brain chimes in.

It doesn't matter, though, does it? The story is out. The damage is done. Her father, my oldest friend, has threatened me, my bank's stocks are down, its clients are ruffled, and my ex-wife is now parading through my halls, all because I lost control and touched this teenager.

Fuck me, I'd touch her again. Seeing her like this, digging through the freezer in almost nothing, small breasts jouncing delectably with her movements, I'd do it again in a heartbeat.

Why, why, why can I not banish my craving for her? She poisons my thoughts constantly. And the memories are even worse, in all their graphic, visceral detail.

Without thinking, I flick the overhead light on and watch her jump back, startled.

"Sneaking around?" My voice carries like silk, spilling off my tongue and spreading out before her. Husky, demanding, flirtatious—exactly how I shouldn't be when addressing Abbie.

Her top is more see-through than I expected, the outline of her deep pink areolas clearly visible through the fabric. In her startled state, she doesn't bother to cover herself, but rather looks torn. Caught. Delicious. Want grasps me so hard around the middle I can barely breathe.

"Cat got your...tongue?" I take in the view shamelessly. The way her top drapes across her breasts, the way her shorts hug her thighs, the center seam of them drawing a line straight down to her sweet cunt, leaving blessedly little to the imagination. I can almost taste her again.

After a brief pause, confidence seems to overtake her. She lifts her chin and bats her eyes, setting the glass of ice in her hand on the counter and coyly twisting her hair around her finger.

"I wasn't sneaking. Just getting a drink. I've been scrolling through all the guys on this dating app. It's thirsty work."

My mouth forms a hard line. "Is that so?" I cross the gap between us and am instantly overwhelmed by the lingering scent of her familiar vanilla body wash, filling my nostrils with pure sex. "Or were you hoping to run into me?"

"I didn't even know you'd be up," she scoffs.

I lift a brow. "Look at what you're wearing."

Her indignation falters just for a second, but I see it. "I'm comfortable in this," she protests, throwing her shoulders back. The fabric pulls taut across her breasts, and that's it.

I'm undone.

Desire takes hold of me and I give into it. Because I want to. Because I can. I slowly reach out and thumb her left nipple with the barest touch, finding it already hard and pebbled and begging for me to suck it right through the silk. My mouth starts to water.

"See?" I murmur and repeat the motion across her right nipple, which is just as perked and ready. "I was right."

"Wrong." That sass I love so much comes out full force. "I didn't wear this for you. It's for the app. A couple guys asked for selfies."

My gut twists with a shock of pure jealousy. No other man is going to see her like this. No one else is going to know what she looks like, tastes like, the sounds she makes as she comes.

"I should grab an ice cube, too, really tease them," she taunts.

I'm so goddamn furious, I'm seeing red. "The fuck you will."

"Oh no?" Her lips form a slight pout. "Are you trying to tell me what to do? You think you own me?"

Without thinking, I pin her against the refrigerator door, watching her chest heave and her eyes beg me to do more than just hold her here. She's baiting me. I know she's baiting me; she's too young and inexperienced to do anything discreetly, like Natasha would.

But I don't care. All I want right now is to take this woman back to my bed and fuck her until she screams. I want her mouth around my aching cock. I want her fingers in my hair. I want her soft moans in my ears. But I can't risk discovery. I can't let any of those things happen.

"Don't ask questions you already know the answers to." The words roll out of my mouth like quiet thunder.

"You threw me away," she whispers.

"You sold me out."

"Bullshit," she hisses. "You know I didn't do it."

With a barely retrained grunt, I reach for the wall and slap off the lights, leaving us in darkness again. Then I dip my head and bite the soft, smooth skin of her shoulder, just enough to leave marks. She gasps, making my cock strain against my briefs.

"I know no such thing," I tell her.

"Then I guess I should hurry up and get back to these silly little boys on my phone. You know—the ones who can admit they want me?" She's breathy, pressing against me, and there is no conceivable way she's leaving this kitchen without my hands touching her body all over.

"I want you. But I don't trust you anymore. Once trust is broken, it takes a long time to heal." I grab the glass off the counter, dig out an ice cube, and run it slowly across her jaw.

Her eyes burn into mine. "I trusted you, too." Her whispers are fierce, strong, tantalizingly angry. I fight off the urge to push her to her knees. "And you betrayed me."

I run my nose against the length of her neck, stealing her breath, savoring the trembling flesh beneath me. "We are at an impasse, then."

"Fuck your impasse."

At this, I drop the glass, grab her arm, and spin her around so her back is against me, my cock pressed against her tight ass. Then I slide the ice cube against her collarbone, listening to her breath catch. I trail it down the center of her chest, then lower, across the small mound of her breast, until the ice hits her nipple and she gasps louder.

"This is why people found out," I murmur in her ear. "You have no sense of propriety. You moan—" I suck on her earlobe and she moans again. "You groan—" I gently rim her nipple with the ice and her hands grab at my sides. "You don't know how to be quiet."

"You like me mouthy," she breathes. "You like it when I'm loud."

"Nonsense." I switch the ice cube to her other nipple. "It's unbecoming."

"You come harder when I'm louder." Abbie presses her ass into my cock, arching her back.

She's not wrong, which only irritates me more. "You don't know me."

"That's a lie." Her voice is soft, but her words are powerful. "I know you better than almost anyone in this house. You showed me a side of you that no one else sees."

"How do you know I'm not just using you?" The ice cube clatters to the floor, both of my hands now full of her nearly-bare breasts. She writhes under me and I long to strip her naked.

"Because the mess isn't worth it." Abbie is suddenly sincere, spinning in my arms to face me, her hands sliding up into my hair. "If you were only using me, I would have been out on my ass the minute you saw those trashy magazines."

"It could still ruin us." My hand drifts down her lower belly, toward the band of her shorts. Abbie stands on her tiptoes to shorten the gap, her body seemingly as hungry as mine.

"It already has."

"Then what are you doing here?" I whisper in her ear.

Abbie guides my hand under her waistband and down into her hot, creamy center. She is deliciously wet and slick, no priming needed. I find her tight little nub and stroke it with my thumb until her whole body shivers.

"I should ask you the same question," she murmurs.

I dip a finger inside her, twisting as I push up and in, and she gasps. I know Abbie needs me to give her more. She doesn't need to say it.

Moving her to the counter, I bend her over with her back facing me and clamp a hand against her mouth, reaching down the front of her shorts again. I begin to fingerfuck her slowly, deep and rhythmic, savoring the hot constriction from this angle. My cock thrusts between her thighs in time, precum soaking through my boxer briefs, and she grinds back against me, trying to stifle her sharp little moans. If I close my eyes, it's almost like we're really fucking.

"You don't get to ask the questions in my house," I growl in her ear. "You don't get to send naughty pictures to horny little boys who don't know how to appreciate your body, much less find your clit."

She turns her head away from my hand so she can talk back. "You don't get to tell me what to do," she insists. Then she reaches back to pull hard on my hair.

It's my turn to groan, losing the battle between enjoying the pleasure of punishing her sweet body and the need to satisfy my own desires.

"I have something you can put in that sassy little mouth of yours."

Immediately, she pulls my hand out of her shorts and drops to her knees. Her hands go straight for my briefs, tugging them down and breaking me free.

"Tell me." Her whispers are hot against my bobbing

cock as she looks up at me, cupping her breasts, pushing them together. "Tell me to do it, Graham, and I will make you come all over this kitchen floor."

I want to take her up on her threats. I want to thrust into her mouth and leave a trail of cum down her chest. I want it to be sloppy and furtive and messy, everything I've dreamt of for the last week. But I can't put my power back in her hands so easily.

Only she will be punished tonight.

Hooking my fingers under her chin, I lead her back to standing and spin her around once more. This time, I lead her to the kitchen island and push her torso flat across it, her body obeying my every move. From here, I could easily fuck her from behind. I could fuck her in her tight little asshole, but then she'd think our relationship is back on again, and I can't have that.

Sliding her shorts down, I push her thighs apart until her cunt is spread open for me. I can see her legs trembling, but it doesn't stop me from tracing a cube of ice from her ankle to the back of her knee, up to her inner thighs, and finally back and forth across her clit.

When the cube is completely melted, I pulse my cold fingers inside her again, until the heat of her pussy warms my whole hand back up.

"Please," she moans softly. "Please fuck me. I'll be quiet. I'll be a good girl. I swear. No one will know."

I think about it. Hard. God knows I could use a release. Instead, I cup her sweet ass, fondling it with the pent-up aggression lusting through my veins. Abbie moans into the island, sticking her ass up higher. I rear back and smack her on the ass soundly, twice.

Then I gather my cock back into my boxer briefs and leave her there, still splayed across the island, her frustration nearly palpable.

If only I wasn't leaving myself just as frustrated as Abbie is.

Chapter Ten

Abbie

HELL. I'm in Hell.

There is no other word to describe it, and it makes all the more sense to me that Graham has always referred to Natasha as the devil—because this is her home, flames and all. I can practically smell the sulfur as she swipes a layer of pale pink eye shadow across my lids.

"You're going to look divine," she purrs. "So lovely."

I'm sitting at the vanity in her room (not Graham's—the only perk of this entire nightmare), trying not to look at myself in the mirror as she makes me up to her satisfaction.

"I feel like this is kind of—"

"Bup, bup, bup," Natasha silences me, tapping me on the nose with a blush brush. "No talking. Your face moves when you talk."

I've seen plenty of videos of celebrities having their makeup done while they talk and laugh and joke, none of which is happening here, but I don't say anything else. Her sickly sweet perfume tickles the inside of my nose as she leans in closer to apply clear mascara to my eyes. I didn't even know you could buy mascara in clear. I'm going to look like a damn twelve-year-old.

This is one way to do makeup, I suppose?

"I bet you can't wait to tell all your friends about this," Natasha goes on, gushing about herself yet again. The woman is absolutely egotistical in a maddening way. "Attending your first night on Broadway with an A-list celebrity. Aren't you just a lucky duck."

Not speaking comes with all sorts of perks, I've learned over the years. I learned to keep silent around my parents, silent around teachers, silent around prodding boys who asked too many questions about my bra size or my interest in their tiny, teenaged dicks. It works just as well on diva actresses who love the sound of their own voice.

"There will be so many cameras and lights, all the paparazzi a girl can handle. But don't you worry. Graham and I will be there to protect you. Have you told your parents yet? Maybe they can keep an eye out for the photos of us and make you a scrapbook." Natasha finishes with my eyes and scoots back to survey her work. "Now we just need a lip color."

I didn't tell my parents about tonight because I didn't want to go. The only person I told was Amanda, crying to her about attending opening night of a Broadway show with the love of my life and his fucking wife. She said I should just enjoy it, since I haven't been to New York to see a show in years, but she didn't seem to understand just how awful it will be. Getting paraded around for the press like an accessory to the Ratliff fairy tale, forced to witness Natasha prancing around in peacock mode while she publicly flaunts the revival of her marriage to Graham.

My heart has been in the pit of my stomach all day.

Natasha uncaps a pale pink lipstick, a hideous color that only someone who doesn't want to look hot would wear, suitable for a fifth grader at Easter, or a freaking nun. It may as well be called Celibacy Carnation. I've never missed my tube of Teenage Fantasy more.

"Beautiful!" she gushes after she applies it, turning my chair so I can see myself in the huge mirror hanging before us. "What do you think?"

What am I supposed to do? Tell my boss-adjacent that this look is atrocious? I know she's made me up like this on purpose. The woman has good taste—and this isn't it. I've seen her done up plenty of times. At present, she's working a sultry, smoky eye complete with winged liner, and a deep red lipstick that makes her look like a classic Hollywood starlet.

Meanwhile, I look like Barbie's wholesome, sexless little sister, Skipper.

"Mm. Stunning." I force a smile. "Thank you so much for helping me."

"It's my pleasure." Natasha pats my cheek lightly and it takes all of my willpower to not recoil under her icy hands. "Now, we need to talk about your wardrobe."

"I brought a dress like you asked. It's the nicest one I have with me." I gesture over my shoulder, where a simple black sheath dress hangs on the bathroom door. It's a little short, I guess, but it's subtle enough not to pull any attention away from Natasha, I'm sure.

"Oh, no no no, dear. That won't do. Don't get me wrong, it's a lovely dress for a night out. But it's far too revealing. We can't have you looking cheap. After all, this is a *Broadway premiere*. It's the highest caliber event you can attend in the city."

She says it like The City is capitalized, like it's the most magical place ever. I've been to New York plenty of times, and always found it a little too loud and a little too gross. Too many people and cars and buildings and smells. Here, there's fresh air and grass and plenty of space to stretch. "The City" makes me feel claustrophobic.

"We look to be around the same size," Natasha says. "I'm sure I've got something just *perfect* for you. Let's see."

My jaw drops as she sashays off. Same size? Natasha is slender and fit, don't get me wrong, but I'm 19 and she's in her 30s. We have completely different body types.

Across the room, she throws open the doors to a wardrobe housing countless dresses, a dreamy treasure trove of sequins, tulle, silk, and beads. I'm drawn like a moth to a flame. Standing before the wardrobe, almost trance-like, I reach out to feel the luxury at my fingertips.

"Oh, no!" Natasha's voice is light, but she smacks my hand. "No touching, please. These are worth more than your life."

"Sorry." Heat colors my cheeks from the reprimand. She acts like I really am twelve, incapable of appreciating fine things or even dressing myself. "They're just so beautiful."

"Only the best for the best," she sings. "But I'm sure there's something here for you, too."

Ouch.

Natasha carefully flips through the dresses, the ones that would surely catch Graham's eye disappointingly sliding past, until she stops at a lavender number that makes my heart sink.

"Ooh, this will be perfect." She pulls it out and carries it to the bathroom. "Hurry, hurry. We don't have much time."

I look at my phone. We're due to leave in ten minutes, and because she spent so much time making me look like a petite clown, there isn't any time to protest the dress. I take it from her and dash into the bathroom to change as an impatient knock sounds on her door.

"Just a minute, darling, the nanny is getting dressed!"

"I have a name," I mutter to myself, hurrying out of my clothes and sizing up the dress she gave me.

It may as well be a maternity dress for all the coverage it has. It's an off-the-shoulder style with a long double layer of ruffles over the chest, an empire waist, and a very full skirt, effectively hiding my tits and my ass while practically drowning me in shimmery fabric. Another double layer of ruffles adorn the bottom hem. This dress emphasizes my youthfulness, and not in a sexy way at all. I look like a poufy, ruffled, purple nightmare.

Add that to my ridiculous makeup and I want to cry. I want to hide. I never want to leave this bathroom or have Graham see me this way.

I'm going to have to be seen in public like this? Somebody just kill me. Kill me now.

"Come on out, darling!" Natasha pounds on the door. "We've got to go!"

Reluctantly, I open the door and am immediately floored by her appearance. She's changed into a gorgeous floor-length gown in a shimmering red that matches her lip color, with a daring neckline that makes her cleavage pop, and a heavy diamond necklace to highlight her collarbone. She looks incredible. Exactly like a celebrity actress should.

I, on the other hand...

"How adorable!" She claps her hands and grabs a black clutch off the vanity. "You look absolutely perfect, and that dress is so summery. Now come on, Graham and Jude are waiting in the car."

I clench my jaw all the way down the stairs, horrified as the staff comes out to see us off. Esmeralda catches my eye and offers a sympathetic smile. I have a feeling she knows exactly what's going on here. Natasha has intentionally made me look dowdy, so Graham will never look at me again.

And he doesn't. His eyes slide off of me like water on a horse's hind and settle on the magnificence that is Natasha. He extends his arm, gesturing for us to enter the limo before he slides in and sits next to his gorgeous wife.

Just a few nights ago, he had his hands down my shorts. Just a few nights ago, he touched me just like he used to before all of this awfulness started: before the rumors, before Natasha came back, before he told me I broke his heart. Never mind mine, and my bystander innocence.

Now Natasha is radiant as the sun, and I am a dying

glowstick. I am a wilting houseplant, and she is a thriving garden, and Graham is the rain sent down to bless only one of us.

The entire ride is miserable. Graham pours champagne in two flutes while Natasha tuts over my age.

"It's a shame that the nanny can't drink, darling," she says. "We could all be celebrating."

She never calls me by my name; it's always "the nanny," like I'm some sort of TV sidekick. Like I lack a personality and autonomy. It's demeaning and humiliating, and Graham says absolutely nothing as he pours some juice into flutes for Jude and I. Not once does he open his mouth and come to my defense, even though he all but fucked me on the kitchen island not three days ago.

Fucked me and left me, just like before, when I was scrabbling for crumbs and desperately vying for his attention. I've lost every bit of ground I had and he's not giving anything back. Instead, he continues to play house with Natasha, the woman he purportedly hates, and lets her treat me like garbage.

I distract myself by showing Jude how to play checkers on my phone, and about two hours later New York swells up before us, full of bright lights and pungent smells and too many people eating hot dogs as they swelter in the summer humidity. Natasha practically vibrates as we come up on Broadway, where the world well and truly explodes. Despite my best efforts, her excitement is contagious. I've never been to a premiere like this. My parents went to a few of Natasha's opening nights in the past, but I was always kept at home. "Adult events," my mother called them.

Well, I'm an adult now—and it's finally my turn. I even forget about this ridiculous dress and this ridiculous makeup, and instead cling to the window to see what other stars are lining the red carpet. Throngs of fans and looky-loo tourists line the streets, cheering and chanting and waving signs. Natasha checks her makeup one last time and starts fussing with Graham's hair.

"It's fine," he protests, but she carries on.

"You look sexy with your hair a bit disheveled," she purrs, continuing to fuss with it until satisfied. "I want everyone to know we're back together, we're deliriously happy, and we look damn good doing it."

The sky starts falling around me. They *aren't* back together. Are they?

"You've always liked a show," he says to her, reminding me again how much history they share.

Before I can wallow any further, the car slides to a stop at the curb and an attendant in a well-tailored black suit opens the door. Flashing lights and sounds assault us, everyone calling for Natasha to look their way. Graham gets out first and extends his arm to her, which she graciously takes.

Natasha becomes this, like, whole-ass other person. She's always had an air of sophistication and grace, but this is like those habits multiplied tenfold. She places a delicate kiss on Graham's cheek and waves like a queen to the crowds as the attendant helps me out of the car, and in turn, I help Jude.

I want to be excited. I want to be thrilled that I'm

here, no matter what the circumstances around it are. And I try. Maybe, just for tonight, I can forget everything leading up to what got us here and just focus on enjoying the ride like Amanda said. Eventually, Natasha will have to go backstage for the show and I can have Graham all to myself for the duration of the performance. But Natasha's little make-under has had the desired effect, and I can't pretend I'm unaware that next to her effortless glamour, I look like a wilting violet. Literally.

I shuffle along behind the Ratliffs, hoping nobody notices me shepherding their daughter, but when we finally reach the busiest area of the red carpet, the paparazzi absolutely lose their minds.

"Natasha! Natasha! Who's the girl?"

"Is this the nanny?"

"It's her, it's the homewrecker!"

We're assaulted by flashbulbs and shouts. I wish a hole would open in the ground right now and swallow me up. I whisper to Jude that we're almost finished, in hopes that she won't hear or understand what the press is asking.

"Is this a three-way situation, Natasha?"

That seems to get through to her right quick, and she whirls in the direction of that last mouthy paparazzo with a haughty glare.

"Don't be ridiculous," she purrs. "I don't share." Then she smiles, leaning her head against Graham's shoulder and stroking his arm. "But now you know how fake that whole made-up story in the tabloids was. As you can see, my husband and I—our family—has never been happier."

Heat crawls up my cheeks and all I can do is look down and focus on adjusting Jude's hairbow. I can feel the bile rising in the back of my throat, but luckily no one approaches me or asks me any questions directly; they're all focused on the glittering star that is Natasha Ratliff.

As they pose for pictures, I pull Jude aside and we stand with the crew people, waiting for the Ratliffs to finish up so the next celebrity can walk by. Natasha waves demurely as she snuggles into Graham, who wraps his big, strong arms around her waist, stealing all the breath from my lungs.

Inwardly, I'm fuming. Screaming. Completely falling apart. Outwardly, I'm keeping a stiff, bland smile pasted on my face. I want to die.

Natasha looks radiant, and the two of them appease every camera and interviewer on the red carpet, making their rounds, promulgating the lie about how happy they are together. Except maybe it's not a lie. Maybe they really are finding their way back to each other.

It all cuts through me like a hot knife, vicious and agonizing, leaving me with only one tiny, miserable consolation: Nobody in their right mind would believe that I, looking like this, could have actually had an affair with Graham Ratliff while Natasha stands at his side looking like that.

Small fucking comfort that is.

Chapter Eleven

Abbie

I SIT ON THE BED, still draped in hideous lavender ruffles, watching the city lights twinkle before me. Somewhere out there is another version of myself, I decide, who is having the summer of her life.

She's dating a cute, kind boy who brings her flowers from a local florist while she's at work at a horse camp. That Abbie spends her breaks watching TikToks and texting Amanda and lays out in the sun soaking up the golden rays and sipping sweet tea on her days off. On weekends, she dances at the eighteen-and-up clubs or stays in for girls' nights with ice cream and champagne. She wears whatever she wants, and her face isn't on the covers of any magazines. In fact, the media doesn't even know her name.

I can almost see it play out in the reflection of the floor-to-ceiling windows of Natasha's Upper West Side apartment. This place only differs from Graham's estate in size, otherwise full of similar tasteful art and sophisticated furniture in a pleasant color palette, drowning out anything remotely uncomfortable. I don't belong here, surrounded by sirens and honking horns and a million lights. You can't even see the stars.

Next to me, Jude's breath finally evens out as she falls into a deep sleep. I tear my gaze from the windows and tuck her in a little tighter. Esmeralda drove down here after the show and offered to stay with us for the rest of the week to cater to the family's needs, but Natasha dismissed her, saying her services wouldn't be necessary. Jude was so excited at the idea of a sleepover, she could barely settle into bed.

I want to scrub off all my makeup and change into comfy pajamas and snuggle up next to her. Tonight was miserable. I thought as soon as Natasha made her way backstage, Graham would be all mine again. Instead, he barely looked at me and barely spoke to me, like I was some sort of pariah in the midst of all the vipers with cameras.

Look at me! I wanted to scream.

He could have at least touched my arm when the house lights went dark, placed a finger on my knee, something to let me know he was there, but he kept himself carefully isolated in our box. During intermission, he ordered me a sparkling water from the attendant and asked if I wanted anything else. I said no. He didn't look at me again after that, not once.

Whereas I spent more time watching his jawline than I did the show.

Oh, the show. It was absolutely magical. Naturally. The songs were soul stirring and the acting was incredible and it was everything a Broadway production should be, right down to Natasha's flawless performance. It should have been the highlight of my summer, one of the more memorable events I'll treasure as I move forward in life. Except I could barely pay attention. I clapped when everyone else clapped, I stood when everyone else stood, and the rest of my evening was dedicated to telepathically begging Graham to just. Fucking. Notice me.

It failed, just like every other plan I've had to lure him back. As awful and discouraging as every other moment between us since those disgusting tabloids decided to blare our story.

Except for the other night in the kitchen. My God, did I dream it? I could have sworn he would be different with me after that. Things seemed to finally be moving in the right direction. And now...this. Was he just using me? Has he been using me all along? Letting me build up this fantasy version of our relationship in my head, just so he can get off when he needs to?

The door cracks open and light slices into my silent haven. "There you are, darling!" Natasha coos, slurring a bit. "I've been looking for you! Everyone wants to meet you."

"I'm watching Jude." The hairs on the back of my neck stand up, and I'm instantly unnerved at her presence. She's obviously been drinking, and she's worse when she's drunk.

"Nonsense. She's dead asleep." Natasha shoves the door open and comes over to grab my arm. "You *must* come meet everyone."

She hauls me through the room, and I only allow it to keep her from waking up Jude. Maybe I can at least find some alcohol, get a little tipsy myself, try to forget this whole night ever happened.

The apartment is full of cast members in various stages of makeup and dress, sharing drinks and laughing. They're going to wake up Jude at this rate, so I close the door tightly behind us and let Natasha trot me out into the lion's den.

Graham is nowhere to be seen. Maybe he's not an after-party kind of guy. Too bad he didn't take me with him.

"Here you go." Natasha shoves a diet soda into my hands. "You look like you need a drink."

I look at the can. I do need a drink, more than ever in my whole life, but not this one. I smile meekly and look around. "Is there something a little...stronger?"

"Oh, heavens no!" Natasha gasps. "I can't have my *nanny* getting drunk on the job. You're just a teenager, after all."

She pats my cheek affectionately, like I'm a toddler. I'm not fooled for a second by her sycophantic PDA. She knows exactly what she's doing. That bitch is loving this.

I jerk back from her pawing. "Actually, I'm—"

"Evelyn!" She's got a death grip on my arm as she hauls me across the living room to a woman I don't recognize. Everyone looks so different in the apartment, away from the bright lights and their full costumes. "Evelyn, here she is!"

"So *you're* the nanny," Evelyn, whoever she is, gushes. "Well, she's just beautiful. How do you do it, Natasha?"

"Oh, she's nothing but a child." Natasha grins with

her shark teeth and doesn't release her grip on me. "You know how rumors are, and those gossip rags are always trying to stir the pot with something preposterous. But Graham and I just pay it no mind. She's positively wonderful with Judey."

"Well, if you ever get bored with the Ratliffs, call me. I've got three littles at home." Evelyn laughs. "And *my* nanny is deplorable. Natty, did I tell you about the time she—"

I have nothing to say as she and Natasha banter for a bit longer, gossiping about their staff, forgetting I'm there, moaning and groaning about how motherhood is so difficult when you have a real career to manage. I sip my soda politely and wait for the second Natasha releases my arm to escape. It doesn't take long, because another cast member calls for her across the room.

"Natasha! We're doing shots! Come, come."

"Oops. Duty calls!" Natasha giggles. "Let's go, Evy. We need to step this party up!"

"I'm too old for shots," Evelyn protests, but dutifully follows Natasha across the apartment, leaving me alone by the window.

In the reflection of the glass, I spy Graham on the other side of the apartment, deep in conversation with an older man. I look over my shoulder and try to catch his eye, but he's so deep in discussion that it doesn't matter. I'm nothing more than scenery here, dragged out here for the sole purpose of assuaging the rumors (and guilt) that the Ratliffs collectively carry.

I'm just here to make them feel better. Assure everyone that I'm an innocent, that the tabloids couldn't possibly have it right. It makes me want to be dangerous.

"You look like you're having fun," a young male voice says behind me. It sounds like he's teasing me in a nice way, which I appreciate after dealing with Natasha's bs.

"Doing my best," I say, turning around with the brightest smile I can manage to meet my mysterious visitor.

He appears to be in his mid-20s, with shaggy, sandy colored hair and brown eyes, giving off a wholesome, down-to-earth vibe for all his boy-next-door handsome-ness. In fact, in his casual khakis and a wrinkled denim button-down, he looks almost as out of place as I do.

"I'm Derek." He grins and extends a free hand. "I'm one of the chorus members in the show. No one fancy, in case you were wondering. Maybe someday."

"Charmed." And I am, completely. He's adorable. I try to channel sophistication despite my hideous dress, even though this outfit makes me want to run and hide. "I'm Abbie."

"The nanny?" he asks.

I can't help jolting back a little. I hate that word now. "Yes."

"Shit, I'm sorry! I didn't mean to relegate you to a nasty title or anything. Natasha's been talking about you all night, that's all. I think she really likes you."

"Does she?" That's a lie and I know it. Natasha is the reason I'm still here, but it's obviously only because I make her and her marriage look better. I wouldn't call that "liking," I'd call it "using." Something she's excep-tionally good at.

"It sounds like it. She's mostly been saying how great you are with her kid. I could never do your job. Don't get me wrong, kids are fun, but all day every day? Whew. You must be some kind of magical Mary Poppins or something."

His smile is nice. It's not laced with poison or deceit, but with genuine kindness.

I have to laugh. "Yeah, maybe. Jude's a cool kid, though. It's not so bad."

Derek nods. "Lucky for you."

We share another smile, and I clink my soda can against his plastic drink cup. It's not the ubiquitous red plastic cup you see at most parties—it's gold. Because of course.

"It's nice to meet someone else in the trench," I tell him.

That gets a laugh out of him. "I hear you. Actors can be a bit...much. Especially this crowd, the whole Broadway thing. But I don't mind being in the trench if it means you're here."

His eyes meet mine and I realize that he's most *definitely* flirting with me. Hell, yes.

Confidence zings through me, bright and hot. It's exactly what I need after that demoralizing red carpet scene earlier, and after being put in my place over and over again by Natasha all night while being completely ignored by Graham.

Not only that, but he's flirting with me despite this atrocious getup. Joke's on you, Natasha. And if I'm lucky, maybe Graham will notice and see what he's missing.

I turn up the wattage on my smile. "So, how'd you end up in New York, Derek?"

He actually blushes, this boy. "Ah, it's embarrassing."

"I'm sure it isn't," I prod.

"Oh, but it is. I'm just your cliché Midwesterner who starred in all my high school plays and moved to the Big Apple right after graduation with stars in my eyes. Only to find myself waiting around for callbacks all day and wondering when my big break is gonna come."

"Ohio?" I guess.

"Indiana," he says, shaking his head dramatically. "Terre Haute, population 60,000. Most famous for being the home of Clabber Girl Baking Powder."

"Oof. I'm so sorry," I say teasingly, patting his arm. I leave it there. Derek doesn't seem to mind.

"It's okay. I'm recovering," he says. Then he leans in conspiratorially. "To be honest, I'm kind of boring at these things. Never been much of a partier. I'm sure you're way more interesting than I am."

I laugh. "Right. I spend my days with the eight-year-old daughter of a billionaire. Don't get me wrong, I love her to death, and she's not a spoiled brat in the least. But it's not like we gallivant around the City. You must have such a fun life, working on Broadway and everything."

"I mean, it is the dream," Derek says humbly. "But everyone wants to make it big here, and most of us live together in tiny roach motel apartments, working our side hustles to survive."

"Side hustles!" I widen my eyes. "Tell me more. What do you do?"

"I'll give you one guess. Don't think too hard."

"Hmm...you've got to be...a waiter. No, a barista! At a coffee shop. In Brooklyn?"

"Cobble Hill." He cracks a cheeky grin. "See? I'm so boring, you could write my biography with your eyes closed."

"I have faith in you," I tell him. "You'll transcend the stereotypes, mark my words."

"I appreciate the vote of confidence. Really." He clinks his glass with mine. "So, are you off the clock? Want a real drink?"

"Oh my God, do I ever. This soda could use a little kick." I lift my half-empty can.

"I think I can help you out with that." He winks at me. "What can I get you?"

"Rum would be great?"

He nods. "Be right back."

Derek disappears into the throng of people. I use the opportunity to look for Graham, but I don't see him anywhere. Well, I can at least enjoy my evening with this cute actor boy. It's not like I'm looking for anything serious, but who doesn't like being hit on at a party?

"The eagle has landed," Derek says, reappearing with a cup of dark rum in his hand.

"You're the best," I gush as I hold out my can and he carefully pours the alcohol into it. "Thank you so much. No one will even know."

"Cheers." His grin is intoxicating, and I think about kissing him, maybe.

I'm in the process of taking a swig from the can when Graham's voice cuts through the general din.

"What's going on over here?"

Derek shrugs casually. "We're just talking—"

"Are you trying to get my underage staff drunk?" Graham looms over him menacingly.

"It's just a little rum," I protest, secretly thrilled I finally caught his attention. Except he's not looking at me, he's only looking at Derek.

"Unacceptable." Graham takes the can from my hand, still refusing to acknowledge me with anything other than his words. "Go to bed, Abbie. You're dismissed."

My cheeks flame with humiliation. "But—"

"Now."

Frustrated and ashamed, I offer a tight smile to Derek, who looks terrified, and make my way to the guest bedroom like a sullen child.

Chapter Twelve

Abbie

GRAHAM PUT me up in a different room from Jude, on the opposite side of the apartment from the rest of the Ratliffs. The privacy is nice, but that's about all I can say for the entirety of the evening. This whole charade has been such bullshit.

He won't look at me, won't touch me, parades around with his arm around his ex-wife, but won't let another boy talk to me? Fuck him.

I curl up on the bed in my pajamas—just a Cornell T-shirt with the university crest on it and a pair of boxer shorts, nothing Natasha wouldn't approve of—and scroll through the various dating apps I have on my phone, looking for something fun. Maybe someone to exchange pictures with. Flirting with Derek, as low-stakes as it was, made me feel good. I could go for more of that to take the edge off my PTSD from this whole ridiculous, awful night.

I try to channel the Abbie I saw in the windows earlier, the one who would happily date one of these boys, but she's not coming. JackSparrow477 with his boat doesn't tickle my fancy. Cody Fisher and his array of fishing poles doesn't either. Nor does PlayaManShawn with his series of shirtless beach volleyball photos. Not a single guy on this stupid app seems even remotely worth my time. Because they aren't. My time has been dominated by more powerful men, and now there's a strict door code.

These boys ain't it.

Derek wasn't all that thrilling either, but he was here and he was nice and he was willing to spike my drink. His availability and proximity to Graham made him appealing. Plus, he was easy on the eyes. There's no point to pursuing that now, though—not when Graham isn't around to witness it and not when his jealousy from earlier did exactly nothing anyway. I'm still tempted to sneak back to the party, though. Anything is better than sitting here pouting over my phone.

Outside in the rest of the apartment, the party rages on. I keep expecting poor Jude to show up at my door, bedraggled and tired, awoken by Natasha's ridiculous theatre friends. But then something shatters and the party dips into silence for just a moment, before Natasha's voice rings out, "It was just a vase, loves, no worries!"

"Yeesh," I mutter, throwing my phone across the bed in frustration. This is all terrible: Natasha's manipulations, Graham's rejection, the party, the lack of booze, all of it.

Heated voices exchange low, muffled words in the hallway outside my door. I can't make out the conversation, but judging by the cadence and tones, it's likely Graham and Natasha. My heart races at his nearness but my anger tamps it down.

I hurry to the door to try to catch the gist of what they're saying, but the voices are gone and now Natasha's voice rings out from the living room, rallying the troops to move the party elsewhere.

"We don't want to wake sweet Judey," she slurs loudly. "Off we go!"

There's a chorus of cheers and groans, and the sound of everyone hustling toward the door. Great. Now there's no one here to entertain me even if I did sneak back out. Guess this evening is screwed. What a freakin' shitshow of a day. Easily the most embarrassing and torturous day I've had in a while.

I crack open the door and watch the party slowly trickle out of the apartment, one big drunk parade. They leave behind a huge mess that the staff is going to have to clean up and my resentment grows. Shattered glass, half-empty cups everywhere, wine spills on the carpet, empty bottles strewn about on tables and chairs. It's like they have no care for the people who work here, or anyone other than themselves.

As soon as the door shuts behind the last person, I climb back into bed with a sigh. Then I return to my apps, thumbing absently through profile after profile, hoping I'll get tired soon, when the door to my bedroom swings open.

Graham stands in the doorway, illuminated by the hall lights, looking dangerous.

"You think you can just flirt with any little boy, do you?" he seethes.

"You think you can just barge in here and ask?" I shoot back, even though I'm already fighting the heat gathering in my center.

I sit up and tilt my head to the side, awaiting his next move.

"Cut the shit," he says, shutting the door behind him. He starts loosening his tie, and my hammering pulse kicks up another notch. "This isn't some sort of game."

"Isn't it, though?" I feel the anger in my throat and the primal attraction elsewhere, tangling into a web of confusion. "You're the one who fingerfucked me in the kitchen and then let your *ex-wife* parade you around tonight like her personal arm candy."

Graham kicks off his shoes and unbuttons his shirt. "Things are complicated right now. You know this."

I try not to watch him undress, because each layer that hits the floor sets me more and more aflame, to the point where it's a struggle to keep my thoughts in order. "I know I didn't go to the press, and you can't seem to accept that. Doesn't seem that complicated to me."

"It's complicated," he repeats. He pulls off his undershirt, revealing his bare chest and flat stomach. My breath catches in my throat. "But you should still know who you belong to."

"*Belong to?*" The words catch me completely off guard. "Excuse me?"

We stare each other down for a tense, charged moment, and then he rushes at me, his hands in my hair and his mouth on mine. I know I should push him away, force him to talk this out with me some more, like grown adults, but fuck it. I'm nothing but a vast, stormy ocean of need as I stroke my tongue against his.

His body presses me down into the mattress and I let myself get lost in his touch, falling into the taste and feel and scent of him, the sound of his groans in my ear, every last inch of him all-consuming. I fumble for his belt and push his pants down as he tugs my T-shirt over my head. The air perks my nipples, but it's his rough thumb raking over them that turns me into a twisted hurricane of want.

I lets out a gasp as Graham dips his head and gently licks my nipple, sending a shock of desire straight between my legs and weakening my resolve even more. I have wanted this man so badly, every single minute of every single day, and I haven't been granted any true relief, only teasing and ever-mounting desperation. So tonight, I'm going to take everything he has to give. But that doesn't mean I'm not going to call him out first.

"You can't just walk around pretending I don't exist and then come into my room and do this," I say, trying to keep the breathiness from my voice, trying to sound more in charge and demanding. That's how he likes me, but I also want answers.

"You mean this?" He leans down and wraps his mouth around my other breast, sucking so hard I have to fight the urge to scream his name. "Or this?" He flicks my wet, swollen nipple, then pinches it so hard I can feel the shockwaves in my pussy.

"Yes, actually," I say, pulling his hair in retaliation. He moans at my roughness and bites down gently on my nipple. Euphoria explodes through me. "You didn't even look at me tonight."

"Lies. I couldn't keep my eyes off you." Graham's voice is husky. His hands gently slide down my rib cage until he reaches my hips, where he hooks his fingers into my boxers. "Even in that ridiculous getup, you looked stunning. Immaculate. Ripe for the fucking."

He pulls off my shorts, leaving me on the bed in nothing but my lacy white underwear, the only item of clothing I actually chose myself for this event. His eyes drink me up.

"Well, you did a fantastic job acting like I was invisible," I tell him with a glare. "Maybe it's my turn to deny *you* now."

"I'd like to see you try," he teases, but his voice is rough and demanding. He traces the waistband of my panties. "Take these off."

"Maybe I want them on."

Graham puts his hands around my throat, gentle enough not to hurt me but firm enough to steal my breath. "I said take them off."

Oh, it's going to be one of those nights. Excitement hums through me as I obey, lifting my hips to shimmy them off, so now I'm completely naked beneath him. My skin glows with the city lights coming in through the window, goosebumps rising from Graham's touch. He rubs his thumb down the side of my neck, a look of intense focus on his face. It isn't pretty, it's hungry.

And then his mouth consumes me. He locks his lips onto mine so hard that I can barely breathe, and the asphyxiation sends bolts of electricity to my center. I surrender fully to his kiss, to the probing of his tongue, to the way he licks the inside of my mouth. He's in control now.

I am his.

With a firm hand, Graham guides me off the bed and turns me around so my ass is pressed against his hot, raging erection. Liquid heat is all my pussy knows and craves. He bends me over the bed and pushes my face into the comforter. Heart racing, I'm panting heavily while I wait for him to take off his underwear. When the tip of his cock brushes my opening, I hiss, losing my mind with anticipation.

"You are mine," he says throatily, words crashing around me like rolling thunder.

"Mmm," I moan in agreement. I can barely think straight long enough to tell him, "I started taking my birth control again."

The way he groans when he allows himself to enter me bare almost undoes me. He thrusts hard and deep, a key in a lock, so fucking perfect I could lose my mind, but then he stops.

"You're all mine," he repeats, his breath hot in my ear. "Do you understand?"

"You can't tell me what to do," I tell him, but it lacks conviction—I'm drunk on the feeling of his cock inside me, and we both know my sass is all for show. "I am my own person."

"I own you," Graham insists. He pulls out almost all the way, leaving me gasping, and then slams back inside so hard I can't stop the little yelp that comes out of my mouth.

He does it again and again, pulling out until I can barely feel his tip inside me, then pounding into me roughly, out and in, hard and deep, slowly withdrawing before slamming right back in. It's hot as hell, but it's such a fucking tease. I need more, so much more. I'm getting hotter with every agonizing thrust, panting and shaking as he punishes me with his cock.

"Fuck me," I beg, tears of need stinging my eyes. "Hard. Please."

He smacks my ass with the flat of his hand. "I own you. I own this cunt. I own these tits. I own this mouth." Every piece of me is punctuated by another thrust, so hard my breasts bounce.

"Tell me again," I pant, so dizzy with lust I have to keep my eyes closed so the room won't spin.

"I own you," he says. "I am it for you. I am the only one you fuck. I am the only one you suck. I am the only one you text naughty pictures to in the middle of the night."

"Yes," I gasp again, his words stirring the monster within me. "You own me."

He smacks my ass again and then grabs my hair painfully, yanking my head back. "Touch yourself. Now. Squeeze that clit while I'm fucking you."

I obey, sliding a hand down between my legs, my fingers finding my slick and swollen nub. He begins thrusting faster and harder, like a fucking machine, just like I wanted, our bodies moving in a tense harmony; it's the roughest sex we've ever had and I am loving it.

I'm so inundated by pleasure and pain, by the sound of Graham's grunts and my desperate gasps, the ache of his fist in my hair and his cock hitting me so deep, the slap of our bodies and the fucking sheer euphoria of it all, that I can't keep my orgasm at bay. It builds so fast that I'm powerless to fight it, so I give myself up to it and let it spill over.

When it peaks, it's harsh and body rocking, a climax as strong as a tsunami wave. I'm shattering, my insides contracting with intense bursts of pure bliss. I try to muffle my cries in the bed, my eyes wet with tears, but Graham starts groaning louder behind me and it's so sexy I can't keep from egging him on.

"Fuck, Graham, don't stop," I moan, panting between the words, still coming down from the orgasm that just rocked my world. "You're so fucking sexy. Fuck me, fuck me, fuck me."

His pumping intensifies, faster and faster, until abruptly he stops, his hands roaming my ass without spanking, like he's trying to keep himself together. I rub myself against him, moaning, trying to push him over the edge, to make him come, and he swears and pulls out.

"Don't leave," I beg.

"Turn over," he snaps. "Open your mouth."

Eagerly, I do as he instructs. I love the feel of his cock in my mouth, hot and wet, and I've been dying to pleasure him this way again. More than anything, I love watching him come apart for me. It makes me feel powerful. Like I'm in control. Because I am.

I take all of him, relaxing my throat the best I can, sucking him hard the way he likes. Graham drops his head back and wraps his hands in my hair again, holding me steady. Then he thrusts into my mouth, slow at first, then faster and harder, until he's groaning and grunting even louder than before. I grab his ass with both hands, urging him deeper into my throat, moaning around his cock, letting him choke me with it. With one last breathless gasp, he finally spills into my mouth, shooting hot spurts of cum across my tongue. I swallow it all down willingly, watching him writhe under my touch.

"*Fuck.*" He pulls back, staring down at me with an intense expression I can't decipher.

I reach for him, wanting more, but he steps back, pulls on his pants, and gathers the rest of his clothes. Then he heads for the door.

"Remember, Abbie"—he turns to look at me before he steps out—"I fucking own you."

"Yes, sir," I whisper, still stretched out on the bed, naked and out of breath.

"Good girl."

With that, he's gone.

Chapter Thirteen

Abbie

Jude and I sit at the breakfast table, eating pancakes and watching her parents do an intricate dance around us as they get ready. Natasha's show is giving a special daytime performance for "some very important people" and Graham dodges questions about his itinerary, which means he's meeting with his lawyer. In my experience, wealthy people who don't want to answer questions are always planning to meet up with their lawyers soon.

Natasha blows Jude a kiss. "I'll see you later tonight, darling."

"Good luck, Mommy."

"Oh, no!" Natasha gasps, her hand going over her heart. "Never wish an actor luck. Always say 'break a leg' instead."

Jude's face screws up in confusion. "But why would you want to break a leg?"

"Yes, Natasha, why *would* you want that?" Graham asks, flashing a bemused smirk over his coffee cup, shoving things into his briefcase with his free hand.

"You hush." She shoots him a nasty look, but turns to Jude with a smile. "That's just what we say in the biz. 'Break a leg.'"

"Okay, well, um, break a leg?" Jude cocks her head to the side and drags a bite of pancake through her syrup.

"Not so much sugar, Judey." Natasha all but shivers. "It's not good for you. Don't want my sweet girl turning into a pumpkin. Okay, I'm off! Ta-ta!"

Jude slowly lowers her fork back to the plate and pushes it away. I shoot Graham a look.

"Eat up, little warrior," he encourages, but Jude is already getting up from the table. Graham swears under his breath, checks his watch, and swears again. "I've got to run. I'll be back in time for dinner."

He kisses Jude on top of her head and dashes out without another word. I can't help feeling disappointed. Once again, he's back to mostly ignoring me. It's like last night didn't even happen. Except there's a delicious ache between my legs that's proof, and I'm relishing it.

Jude's chair sliding across the floor jolts me out of my head. She stares at me quizzically and I give her a warm smile.

"So! What should we do today? Your school is here, right? We could see if any of your friends want to hang out."

Jude sulks. "They're all away on vacation."

"Okay, well, what kinds of things do you like to do for fun during the school year?" I prod. "You must know Manhattan pretty well."

"Not really. My mom and dad are usually too busy to take me out. Besides school, I mostly just go to my lessons. I've been on class trips to the big museums, but they're just okay. My school took us to Ellis Island and the Statue of Liberty last year, too. It was cool."

My jaw drops. "But...your parents don't take you out for fun when you're here? What about the funky shops on Bleecker Street in the Village? Or the New York Public Library, where they keep the original Winnie the Pooh bear? Ess-a-Bagel? The red velvet cupcakes at Magnolia Bakery? What about the Harry Potter Butterbeer Bar across from the Flatiron Building?"

She just shrugs. "They work a lot." She takes her plate to the sink and then walks over to the bank of windows in the living room. "That's Central Park down there. Have you seen it?"

"Yup." I join her, resting a hand on her shoulder. "It's actually the most filmed location in the world. You know, there are free outdoor concerts there all summer long."

Jude's eyes widen and she presses her nose to the glass to look out at it. "I've been to the Central Park Zoo, but that's it. The park is so huge, I don't think you can ever see it all."

"Well...we could take a carriage ride through it," I tell her. "Just like in the movies."

This time, Jude's jaw drops. "With real horses?" she all but squeals.

This makes me laugh. "Of course, with real horses. What else do you think pulls a carriage? Cinderella's mice?"

"Cinderella's mice turned into horses." Jude looks up at me. "But I can see why you'd be confused."

"Oh my God." I pretend shove her away from me and laugh. "You're the worst sometimes, Jude Ratliff."

This tickles her to no end.

"Come on. Let's hurry up and get ready so we have time to go to FAO Schwarz and Macy's and take a carriage ride through Central Park on the prettiest horses you'll ever see."

"I think our horses are the prettiest horses you'll ever see," Jude says very seriously, but she starts running toward her bedroom. "But let's do it! What's FAO Schwarz?"

"What have they done to you, seriously?" I gape, following her to make sure she picks out something sensible. "The City is your home turf. A kid of your status should know all the best spots."

"What does that mean?" Jude's face scrunches up as she digs through her suitcase.

"I mean, you should be super used to being here."

"No, 'a kid of my status.' What does that mean?"

"Hm." I sit on the bed and watch her sift through her clothes until she settles on a cute lacy dress. Does this kid not know that she's filthy stinking rich? How do you explain that to an eight-year-old? "I guess I mean that a kid whose parents have multiple homes in New York City, like yours. Those kinds of kids generally have the opportunity to see a bit more of the world than other kids do."

"You mean someone whose parents are rich," Jude says.

"Well...yes."

She chews on her lip a minute.

"Does that bother you?" I ask carefully, hoping I haven't struck a nerve. "Knowing your parents are rich?"

"No. For me it's just...normal," she answers candidly. "Aren't your parents rich, too?"

"Um. Not really. Not anymore." This quickly escalated to an awkward conversation.

"So do you get upset that I'm rich and you're not?"

I laugh off the question because I'm not sure how to respond. "Of course not! People everywhere have different amounts of money. The most important thing is to try to have a good life and be a kind person, whether you're rich or not. And if you do have a lot of money, and you can use it to help other people, that's pretty great too."

She nods, mulling it over. "Makes sense." She holds up her dress. "Can you help me with the zipper?"

I help Jude into the dress, and she's beaming when I lead her over to the mirror on the closet door. She does a twirl and spreads her arms. "What do you think?"

"You'll be the prettiest girl in New York City," I tell her. "I love it."

"That's not true." Jude shakes her head. "I think you're the most beautiful girl in the world. And the nicest."

"Aww!" I press my hands over my heart, genuinely taken aback. "I think that's the sweetest thing anyone has ever said to me. You're pretty wonderful yourself, kid."

She looks away, her cheeks going pink. "Thanks."

"Now, then. I think I'd better change if you're going to wear that, what do you think?"

Jude looks at me and nods. "Good idea. We can be dress-up buddies together."

"Deal."

We go to my room and I ransack my overnight bag for something decent, finally settling on a floral silk blouse and a pencil skirt. It's no princess dress, but it's dressy enough.

"Why don't you wear one of my mommy's dresses again?" Jude says, eyeing the clothes I just set out on my bed. "She won't mind."

Ha. She absolutely would mind. And she'd eat my head for lunch. I shake my head with a smile. "This will be dressy enough. I'll wear my strappy gold sandals and some jewelry and I'll look like a million bucks. Promise."

I change quickly in the bathroom.

"So, where is this Effayo store?" Jude asks.

I laugh. "FAO Schwarz. It's in Rockefeller Center, and it's the best toy store in the world. They have everything you could dream of there."

"I dunno, I can dream of a lot. Do they have life-size horse stuffed animals?"

"Probably."

"Wait, seriously?" Jude's eyes go as round as saucers. "I could seriously get a stuffed horse as big as Desi?"

"I mean, I don't exactly have the catalog on hand, but yeah, probably."

"Let's go!" She grabs my arm and hauls me through the apartment. "Come *on*, Abbie!"

"Okay! Okay!" I laugh and peel her little claws off my wrist to hold her hand. "It's not going anywhere, and we have all day."

Jude turns around and gives me a very serious stare.

"Right, right. Horses are serious business. Forgive me, milady." I sweep my arm out as I bow. "After you."

She talks nonstop about the toy store on the entire elevator ride down to the lobby. I stop by the concierge desk and ask for a horse-drawn carriage to take us there, which makes Jude just about lose her mind.

"We can take a horse *to* the horses?" She gapes. "This is the best day ever!"

"That's New York City for you. Horses on horses on horses. And we'll save Central Park for last, since it's so close to your mom's apartment. Maybe if you're lucky we can get real New York hot dogs for dinner and catch some live music while we walk around."

"And real New York pizza, too?"

"Anything you like."

"Yes!" Jude pumps her fist, which makes me laugh.

Just then, a squeal of delight escapes her mouth as a bright white and gold carriage rolls up in front of the building, pulled by one of the biggest black horses I've ever seen in my life.

"It's a Percheron!" Jude all but yells. "Abbie! Abbie! It's a real live Percheron!"

"Well come on, silly, let's go meet him!"

"Oh my God oh my God oh my God," Jude gushes. "I've never seen one in real life!"

Jude takes off, beating me out to the curb. A sweet old man in a gray suit tips his hat at us. "Are you the Ratliff ladies?"

Warmth spreads through me, because I have never in my life wanted to be a Ratliff lady more than I do at this moment. I want to be a part of the club so badly it hurts. Graham said he owns me, that I'm his, so that practically makes me one of them, right?

"Yes!" Jude squeals. "Is your horse a Percheron?"

"You've got a great eye!" The old man claps his hands before climbing down to help Jude into the carriage. "You must really love horses."

"More than anything in the entire world," she tells him.

She's gushing like Ol' Faithful out here. I climb up beside her and get us settled in the warm leather seats. It's hot out, and the horse reeks of manure, but Jude doesn't seem to care one iota. She's curled up in the seat closest to the driver, asking him approximately one million questions about the horse.

"Where am I taking the Ratliff ladies today?" he asks when Jude finally stops to breathe.

"FAO Schwarz!" She looks to me to make sure she said it right. When I nod, she lets out an adorable little "Yess!" and settles into her seat.

Then off we go, us Ratliff girls, to take on New York City.

Chapter Fourteen

Graham

"She didn't sell the story?" I stare in disbelief at the stack of papers on Elise Bowen's desk, detailed written reports submitted by the PI she hired for me. "You can't be serious."

"You really thought she did, and you kept her around anyway?" Bow reclines in her chair and smirks at me. "You sure there's no truth to this story?"

"Bow." I give her a look, but she shrugs.

"No judgment from me either way, I told you that. You're both adults."

"So who the fuck is this Quinn Dempsey?"

"Stable hand. Works under Cassie Ko. It sounds like he and Abbie had some kind of relationship, friendly or otherwise. Either she told him some wild-ass stories or he got jealous and made some up, but whatever the reason, my detective tracked the story back to him."

"Stable hand?" My thoughts are running a mile a minute. I thought I knew everyone on my staff, but my list of employees is extensive. Do I really know every single person who shovels shit in that barn? Hardly. I know Cassie well because she gives my daughter lessons and she's been around for years. But this Quinn guy...

"Fuck," I mutter. "So this little shit is the leak."

Was he the boy whose date I interrupted, all those weeks ago? The one whose job I threatened if he didn't get the fuck out of there immediately? Way to go, Ratliff. Maybe it was me who set him off, made him hungry for revenge.

"I guess someone is getting fired," Bow muses, lifting her coffee mug to drink deeply.

"I'll kill him."

She almost spits out her sip. "Graham, please. As your attorney, I have to recommend that you don't do that. I don't want to be fighting any assault charges, either."

"As your employer, I have to recommend that you fuck off."

"*Client*," Bow emphasizes with another smirk. "But I get the gist."

"I've been treating her like garbage this whole time." I recline in the chair and rub the bridge of my nose. "And Natasha has been all over her like a goddamn praying mantis."

"I always thought those were peaceful insects?"

"They eat the heads of the poor fucks they mate with once they get their jollies off. Cruel beasts, that lot." Not unlike Natasha, who would absolutely eat my soul the second she was given a chance. She wants my bank account, my house, my staff, my child. And she thinks I can't see exactly what she's doing. "I need to get going. Thanks for the answers, Elise."

"Money well spent, I hope." She smiles, rising from her chair to see me out. "Take care, Graham. I'm here if you need me."

I spend the rest of the day attending to business and meeting with colleagues, trying my best to focus on anything but Abbie. By the time I'm halfway through my to-do list, I realize it's past dinnertime.

The whole ride back to Natasha's apartment, I sit in the back of a private car and turn over the new information I got from Bow. This bloody prick ruined my life, and for what? Spite? Abbie is mine and mine alone, and this kid thought he could move in and take what's rightfully mine? I consider calling Ford, getting his advice on how to tank this bastard's entire life, but think better of it. That'll just open up another conversation I'm not ready to have.

What I need to do is talk to Abbie. I don't like to eat crow, but in this case, I owe her the lot of it. I've made her life miserable in the house, barely spoken to her, took advantage of her when I needed release, and I never even gave her the benefit of the doubt. I really am a shit.

I make it back to Natasha's place before anyone else, which is a relief. I can't deal with my ex-wife's nonsense right now. I need to figure out a way to make it up to Abbie, to make things right. She deserves better than the way I've treated her. But how the hell do I fix this?

It's strange to feel like this. Indebted. To feel I've dishonored someone unfairly. This isn't my way. I don't take shit, but I also don't dispense cruelty to those who don't deserve it.

Until now, it seems.

"Daddy!" Jude's delighted voice echoes in the entryway as she and Abbie return from their outing. Behind her, Abbie lugs in a stuffed horse the size of Jude. "Look what we found! FAO Schwarz sent it to Mommy's concierge so we could walk around Central Park without carrying it. That's where we just were."

"Oh really?" I say, scooping her up in my arms. But Jude's so full of energy that she wriggles in my arms like a fish, and I have to quickly put her down.

"Yup! We got pizza and saw Belvedere Castle and heard a real live jazz band! Oh, but first we went to this chocolate place called Jacques Torres. Have you ever had *orange* chocolate? Yeah, me neither. Isn't she the best stuffed animal you ever saw, though?"

Jude gestures at the horse Abbie is carrying.

"Wow," I say. "That thing is...massive."

"She's as tall as me!" Jude crows. "I named her Sugar Cube. I know Mommy says those names for horses are ridiculous, but I really liked it and Abbie said I could name her whatever I wanted, and I wanted to name her Sugar Cube."

"Abbie is right, you can name her whatever you want."

Abbie looks slightly taken aback, and then tries to hide her smile. "I think Sugar Cube is a great name, Jude."

"It is the best name ever for the best horse ever. And Daddy, we got to ride in a *carriage pulled by a real horse* through New York City! It was a Percheron! It was so big and black and beautiful and his name was Mr. Magoo and I didn't get why that was funny even though Abbie tried to explain it. I can't believe they didn't choose something better like Blackberry or Noir. Did you know *noir* means black in French? Percherons are French horses, so that would make more sense than Mr. Magoo."

I just stare as the words spew from my daughter's lips. She hasn't talked this much to me in...months. Abbie has a bemused look on her face as she bustles around in the linen closet and gets a bath ready for Jude, as though this level of chatter was perfectly normal.

Is it perfectly normal for Abbie? Does my daughter adore Abbie that much, that she acts so completely differently around her nanny than she does around her own parents?

An unsettled feeling sits in the pit of my stomach.

"They wouldn't let me ride Mr. Magoo, though. They said he wasn't really a riding horse anymore, and that he just pulls carriages, and that made me really sad. Horses are meant to be ridden and I am meant to ride them."

"We've only been here a few days. You really miss riding that much?" I ask, finally catching a moment to speak.

"More. Than. Anything." Jude sighs dramatically and clings to the neck of her new stuffed horse. "Horse people aren't meant to be kept in the city. Right, Abbie?"

"That's right." Abbie grins at her, and the way she looks at my child puts a strange pressure in my chest.

"I'll see what I can do about that," I tell Jude.

"Okay, good," she says. "New York is nice and every-thing, but it's still summer vacation and the horses prob-ably miss me a lot."

"I'm sure they do. And on that note, it's time for your bath and then bed," Abbie tells her.

Jude looks to me with pleading eyes. "Daddy, can't I stay up just a little while longer?"

"It sounds like you've had a very full day. Don't you want to give Abbie the night off?"

"*Fine.*" Jude sighs heavily, then turns to Abbie. "Can you put Sugar Cube on my bed?"

"Of course!" Abbie smiles brightly and hauls the massive toy into the back bedroom.

Once Jude's in the bathtub under a pile of bubbles, I go to the kitchen to pour myself a drink and stare out at the city skyline.

The night I met Natasha, I thought everything in my life had finally aligned perfectly. It was like flint met steel, sparks turned to flame. I felt invincible, more alive than I ever had.

And yet.

Fire like that burns hot and bright, but it never lasts, does it? It also has the power to destroy everything in its path before it finally starts to fizzle, leaving nothing but blackened ash and catastrophic loss in its wake.

With Abbie, though, it's completely different. It's not that we lack electricity, it's that there's so much more to it than that. Because in her presence I also feel...assured. Confident, powerful, but also...without fear that I'll be subject to the unexpected scorpion sting of her poison later, whether earned or not. She is nothing like Natasha, and I relish it.

There's no question that Abbie can care for my daughter, that she has the child's best interests in mind and that she genuinely adores Jude. I trust this woman with Jude's life. But that isn't all of it, is it? Somewhere, buried inside me, is the sense that I can also trust Abbie with my own life. She's a good person, through and through, and I—I care for her. Deeply.

I'm hit with remorse that I let myself doubt her intentions, even for a second. And I refused to listen to her protestations of innocence. It's almost as if I *wanted* her to have betrayed me, so I could cast her off as just another backstabbing female before I became too attached. Before I got in too deep. Though if I'm honest with myself...it's too late for that. Abbie Montgomery isn't just some fling, no matter how hard I try to convince myself otherwise.

Oh, Ratliff. You are well and truly fucked, old boy.

I ponder all of this over a second glass of whiskey while Abbie finishes getting Jude bathed and ready for bed, trying to unknot the emotions flooding through me. I owe Abbie a lot, and I've got a long way to go in order to make it up to her.

Finally, Abbie comes down the hall, looking tired but cheery, and maybe more than a little tentative. Can I blame her?

"She's asleep?" I ask.

"Out cold. Didn't take long, after the day we had." Abbie smiles, tucking a golden strand of hair behind her ear. God. She really is breathtaking. "Though I'm sure she'll be back to her little firecracker self by breakfast tomorrow. I think that horse of hers is taking up more room in the bed than she is."

A smile plays across my lips. "I don't doubt it."

I take another sip to fortify myself and gesture for her to sit across from me at the table. Abbie takes the seat, still looking a bit apprehensive.

"I spoke with my attorney today. She had a private investigator look into the leak."

Abbie doesn't say anything, but I see the indignation in her eyes. She knows she's innocent. She's known she was innocent from the start. I just refused to listen.

"And?" she finally says, tilting her head.

"And I know you didn't do it," I say.

"Imagine that," she says, her tone uncharacteristically laced with sarcasm. "It's almost like I was telling the truth all along."

"I know. I was awful." I gently place a hand on her knee. "I was...wrong. I should have believed you, Abbie. But it won't happen again—that is a promise. Moving forward, I'll always give you the benefit of the doubt, if you'll grant me the same courtesy. Because I do want to move forward. I want to..." The words die in my throat. I'm not good at apologies.

"Want to what?" Abbie prods gently.

"Do this," I whisper. I cup her cheek and lean in for a kiss. Not a fierce one, where I claim her, as I have on other nights, but a soft kiss that echoes the apologies on my tongue I can't bring myself to say.

"Oh," she breathes when I finally pull back. She's quiet for a moment. I slide my drink over to her and she takes a small sip. "So...what does this mean? Where do we stand now?"

"I don't know," I say honestly. "I wish I could give you every reassurance, but they'd be lies. Because I don't know what happens next. And the last thing I want is to lie to you."

She nods. "Okay."

"Maybe we can just...take it as it comes?" I ask. "Give this thing a chance. See where it goes. My intentions are not dishonorable."

Abbie goes quiet again, seeming to mull it over. Then she looks up at me, searching my gaze. "All right. We can try. I...trust you."

"And I you," I say, taking her hand in both of mine. "Don't worry. I'll figure this out. I'll handle everything."

Just then, the front door opens and Natasha calls out, "Graham?"

I don't take my eyes off Abbie, who suddenly looks terrified. I give her hand a squeeze and then release it. "In the kitchen, Tash."

My ex stumbles into the room, pausing in the doorway. "Well, isn't this cozy?" she slurs.

"We've been discussing Abbie's day out with Jude. The girls took a horse-drawn carriage all over town and—"

Natasha waves me off with a snort. "I'm sure I'll hear all about it from Judey in the morning. I am her mother, after all."

"Of course," I say smoothly, reaching for Abbie's knee under the tablecloth. "By the way, I'll be taking Jude and Abbie back to the estate tomorrow. Jude misses her horses, and I know you've got a full week of shows. We'll be back after the weekend."

Abbie whips her head at me in surprise. I give her knee a light squeeze. The weekend will be the perfect opportunity to make this whole fiasco up to her, and also give me the chance to interrogate and fire the fuck out of Quinn Dempsey.

Natasha's eyes shift between me and Abbie. "For someone who isn't fucking the nanny, you do seem to enjoy spending all your time with her."

I shoot my ex-wife a withering glare. "Drink some water before you go to bed, Natasha."

She sneers at me, but goes to the sink and rummages around in the cupboards for a glass. "How's Bowen doing, by the way?"

My fingers slide up Abbie's thigh, under her pencil skirt, and find her center. She's hot, and I'm sure very wet under her panties. I press gently against her and watch her eyes flutter.

"She's fine," I say casually. "She found the leak."

Natasha stares out the kitchen window as she fills her glass. "Did she?"

"Her private investigator did, yes."

"Given Abbie's presence here, I assume this clears the nanny from the suspect list, then?"

"It does."

Under the table, I move the fabric of Abbie's underwear aside and slip a finger into her, watching her go still as her breath catches in her throat. Her cheeks redden as I slowly pump into her, curling my finger to stroke the soft pad of her G-spot, but she keeps deliciously silent. I cannot wait to have her in my hands once again.

"How delightful." Natasha sounds bitter, but she always sounds bitter, doesn't she? She's lucky her own name didn't come up in the investigation.

I watch her drink her water, my eyes on her, while I discreetly finger Abbie the entire time. She's getting wetter by the second, her thigh trembling, and I wonder if it would be possible to make her come like this, with Natasha standing just a few feet away.

With a clunk, Natasha drops her empty glass in the sink and whirls around with a scowl, realizing she won't get anything more from me. "Well. Good night, then."

Turning on her heel, she stalks off to her bedroom.

Abbie's head dips low as she lets out a long sigh. I withdraw my hand and lean over to place a kiss on her neck.

"Soon," I whisper.

Chapter Fifteen

Abbie

"LET'S GOOO!" Jude bounces around on her bed. "I wanna go *now*."

"We're leaving soon," I assure her, laughing at her craziness. "Trust me, I wish we could be gone right now, too."

"So why aren't we?"

"Your dad has a few things to tie up here in the city before we go."

"Ugh." Jude throws herself backwards onto her pile of pillows and groans. "That means it's going to take forever. Forever, Abbie!"

"It'll be fine," I tell her, but inside I'm just as anxious to leave. NYC has really taken it out of me. I've had a long, hectic day playing tourist with Jude and enough awful encounters with Natasha to last a lifetime, while things with Graham have been a fucking roller coaster.

But it's all been worth it, because now we have an understanding. And I know that he finally believes me. He won't tell me who the leak is, which is infuriating, but

I don't think it's Esmeralda anymore—and he didn't call out Natasha either, which means it likely wasn't her...I think. Unless that's why we're leaving, under the guise of getting Jude back to her horses?

"Do you think Desi misses me?" Jude rolls over on her stomach and picks at the comforter.

"Absolutely," I reassure her, smoothing her wild hair. "In fact, the second we get home, we can go right to the stables so you can see her."

"Okay." Jude looks at me very seriously. "And can we ask Cassie about setting up some trail rides?"

"Of course. We'll go on all the rides and picnics your little heart desires," I promise.

I poke at her and she giggles. "Desi will never know you left."

Her face falls a little. "Are you sure she won't be upset with me?"

"Oh, Jude." I suppress a laugh and throw my arms around her. "None of the horses will be mad at you. They're going to be so happy to see you back in the stables, I promise."

She chews on her lip. "I hope you're right."

"Aren't I always? Now. You need to finish packing your bags so we can head right out once your dad gets back, okay? Chop-chop."

"Ugh." Jude heaves a big sigh and rolls out of bed, flinging open her suitcase dramatically. "This day is going to take forever."

"It'll go faster once you start packing." My phone buzzes in my pocket and I sneak a look. It's my dad. For once, I'm not dreading that I have to answer his call, because I actually have good news for him. "I need to call my dad back, okay? Get packing. I mean it."

"Do I have to? I have so many clothes there. Aren't we coming back after this weekend?"

"Yes. And if you really want to leave your things here, that's up to you, I guess. But then we'll have to leave poor Sugar Cube here all alone, and—"

"No!" Jude shrieks. "I'll pack! I'll pack!"

"Good." I pat her on the head and hurry back to my room to dial my dad's number.

"There you are," he answers after the first ring. "Busy day?"

"We're heading back to the estate for the weekend."

"Oh?" By the tone of his voice, I can tell I've piqued his interest.

"Jude misses her horses. And it seems like Graham's had more than his fair share of quality time with his ex-wife."

Dad laughs. "I can only imagine."

I can't tell if he's insinuating something about Natasha's shittiness specifically or about wives in general, but I don't ask him to clarify. "Anyway, there've been some developments since we last spoke."

"I should certainly hope so."

"Graham's lawyer hired a PI to investigate the leak," I tell him, lowering my voice.

"Smart move. They find anything?"

"Yeah. What I've been saying all along, Dad. I didn't do it." I quickly peek out the door to make sure Jude isn't lurking nearby, and then drop back down on the bed.

"Well, I'll be damned." He lets out a low whistle.

"Congrats on getting your name cleared. This'll go a long way toward patching things up with Graham. Guess you lucked out."

My temper flares. "Luck had nothing to do with it!" I hiss. "I was telling the truth."

"All right, all right. Calm down. So who leaked to the press, then?"

"I don't know," I admit. "Graham won't say."

"Huh. Maybe it was the wife after all."

"*Ex-wife*," I remind him.

"Regardless. If it was her, could be he's keeping quiet about it while he circles the wagons. Getting ready to launch some kind of legal attack. He could even sue her for defamation, scrape a couple million off her divorce settlement. She won't know what hit her."

Dad sounds impressed at the prospect of this plan; I can hear the admiration in his voice. But just because he would take down Natasha like that doesn't mean that Graham would. In fact, in a lot of ways, he and my dad are opposites. Graham is intimidating, sure, but he has moral standards. Whereas sometimes my dad acts like he thinks he's in the mafia. I learned that very early on. Once, a boy tried to spread rumors about me in fifth grade. I told my dad and he said he'd take care of it. I still don't know exactly what he did, but no one talked to me for the rest of the school year.

Still, I wonder if he's got it right about Graham planning a legal coup. I certainly wouldn't mind seeing Natasha crash and burn.

"Well, whoever it is, Graham told me he'd handle it," I say.

"I'm sure he will," Dad says. "So has he apologized to you?"

My cheeks flush hot at the memory of Graham fingering me under the table the night before, right in front of his ex-wife.

"Yes. More or less."

"Good. Does this mean things are progressing?"

"Dad, he only just found out it wasn't me. And we're still stuck in New York at Natasha's apartment. We haven't exactly had any time alone." It's partially true.

"You need to get Natasha out of the picture, Abbie."

"I know! I'm working on it."

"Work harder."

"I'm not a freaking magician! You know how she is. She's everywhere and she has everyone wrapped around her little finger."

"You can do it. I have full faith in you," he says brusquely.

"Thanks, Dad."

I mean it, even though this conversation, like every other one with my father, leaves me filled with frustration. He didn't seem to care that my name was cleared—all he's interested in is making sure his plan to save our family comes to fruition. Nothing I do ever seems to be good enough for him.

After we hang up, I take a quick peek into Jude's room and find her only halfway packed, seemingly distracted by the quiet conversation she's having with Sugar Cube about her plans for the weekend, which include copious trail rides.

"Just wait 'til you see my room!"

I wish I had her optimism for everything. True, Jude is often morose around her parents, but I know her as a different child. A bright, happy, imaginative kid who loves horses more than people and just wants to ride all day until her heart is full. It'll be good to get back to the estate.

Tiptoeing back down the hall, I decide to go to the kitchen and see if I can scrounge up some snacks for the long drive back upstate. But I pull up short when I find Natasha sitting at the table with a pile of newspapers and magazines, all turned to the arts and entertainment sections. She's got a glass of clear liquid in one hand and a highlighter in the other. I'm not naïve enough to think it's water. Natasha has a lot of habits, and all of them involve inebriants.

She must feel my eyes on her, because she looks up and narrows her eyes. "What are you doing in here?"

"I thought I should find some snacks for Jude. For the road." I gesture to the cabinets, but don't make a move toward them. Natasha looks like she's ready to pounce, and I don't want to get any closer to her than necessary.

"Shouldn't you be gone already?"

I shake my head. "We're still waiting on Graham."

"*Mr. Ratliff*," she snaps. "The staff call him Mr. Ratliff, and so should you. Believe me, child, you're no different."

Anger flares through me, but I do my best to bite my tongue. "Well, 'Mr. Ratliff' has business to attend to before we go."

"I don't need you to tell me what my husband is doing."

140

"I thought he was your ex." I can't stop the words from flying out of my mouth. I stand there, a little taken aback by my own insolence, as Natasha stares me down, murder on her lips.

"And you're just the *fucking nanny*," she hisses. "Have you forgotten your place?"

"No more than you've forgotten yours." I can't help myself. I've been shoving back my hatred of her for weeks, gritting my teeth while she talks down to me, smiling when I want to scream, acting like I don't notice when she's insulting me with her backhanded compliments or making snide remarks, and now that the floodgates are open, there's no turning back.

Natasha lets out a harsh, humorless laugh. "You really are pathetic. Oh, I've seen the way you look at my husband. I'm not stupid. I recognize those longing gazes, the way you stick out your itty-bitty tits when he's around. I can smell your desperation, and it stinks. But you'll never have what I have."

My ears are ringing as rage churns in my gut. "What's that? A mediocre career and a coke habit?"

She stands up so fast, her chair falls backwards. "What did you just say?"

I have two options here—fight or flight. My heart is practically pounding outside my chest, but I swallow down my fear and stand my ground. I can't move forward with Graham if she's around. It's time to officially throw down the gauntlet. "You heard me."

Natasha stalks across the kitchen so fast, I don't even have time to register that she's pulling her arm back until I feel the impact of her hand slapping me hard across the face, with so much force that my head rocks back.

My palm immediately goes to my cheek, which is hot and tingling despite my shock.

"Don't you *ever* forget your place, you ungrateful little bitch. You think I don't know about your family's embarrassing financial troubles? Oh, yeah. I know all about it. Daddy's broke because Mommy spent all his money, and his business is failing so bad he forced you to get a full-time job for the summer. I know you're desperate for scraps because you've got nothing left. You have *nothing*, and your family is nothing. So don't you dare speak to me like that ever again, or I'll make sure you never step foot on Ratliff property again."

Tears well up in my eyes, but I blink them back and try to steady myself. Natasha grabs my face, her nails digging into my stinging cheek, and then leans in so close I can smell the vodka on her breath.

"Fucking try me," she hisses.

All I can do is nod meekly and then bolt, hurrying down the hall back to my room.

As soon as I slam the door shut, a hysterical little laugh escapes me. My cheek still throbs, but a feeling of victory pumps through me. I did it. I got to her. I really, truly got under her skin. Natasha Ratliff is losing her boundaries.

Is it a good sign, or a bad one?

Chapter Sixteen

Graham

THE FURTHER AWAY THE car takes us from New York City, the easier it is to breathe.

I should have stayed at the estate.

There are a lot of things I should have done, a lot of people I should have been kinder to. By people, I mean Abbie and especially Jude. My kind, brilliant, sensitive, horse-loving child.

Her head rests heavily on my shoulder as she dozes, and I drop a kiss on her hair before returning to the view outside my window. My daughter is the light of my life— the one thing I'm most proud of, more than any business deal or banking empire or pile of stocks and bonds. Because Jude is good to the core, entirely pure of heart, and far and away my very best work.

So why have I treated her so terribly since Natasha left us? My God. I've pushed her away time and again, burying myself in my job and my liquor bottles in futile attempts to hide from the nightmare my life had become.

And then, wracked with guilt, I'd turn around and try to make it better, overcompensating for the time I'd spent away from her, spoiling her, showering her with gifts and pet names and trying to fix my mistakes—only to immediately disappear into my laptop and my whiskey again. I'm sure by now I've given the poor thing emotional whiplash.

What kind of father am I to do such a thing to my child? Intentional or not, I've been a monster. Between me and Natasha, that poor child is going to need years of therapy to recover. And I would know.

My own father left me a total wreck after a childhood spent in a series of boarding schools, my holidays passed with distant cousins of my deceased mother while Father was busy entertaining important rich people on his yacht. The only physical sign of affection I can recall ever receiving was a clap on the shoulder when I graduated from university. Up until that point, I lived in fear of disappointing him, and even now it haunts me sometimes —the worry that I'll never live up to his expectations, no matter how much success or wealth or stature I acquire.

I suppose it's no wonder that I struggle to make the right choices when it comes to Jude—my own father was no kind of role model, and my ideas about healthy emotional attachments and raising children and forming strong family bonds are educated guesses, at best. But that's no excuse. I need to do better. I *will* do better. I owe it to Jude.

This weekend, I've decided, will be full of amends. My relationship with Jude isn't the only one that needs repairing—Abbie deserves reparations as well. And I'm going to fire the fuck out of that stable hand, perhaps bash in his kneecaps while I'm at it, and my excitement at the prospect is palpable. It's been a long time since I've punished someone with my fists, and I find the thought delicious. Nobody fucks with Graham Ratliff like he has and gets away with it.

I suddenly tune into the sound of Jude's voice and realize that she's chatting with Abbie now. I've missed most of the conversation. We've just turned down the drive of the estate.

"I bet Cassie missed me, too," Jude is saying as the house swells before us on the horizon. "And Esmeralda. Why didn't Mommy let her stay?"

"Because Esmeralda was needed at home, love," I remind her. "But I'm sure everyone's missed you a great deal."

"Who wouldn't?" Abbie asks. "You're always such a delight, Jude."

"I know." She beams. "Daddy, Abbie says we can have as many trail rides and picnics as I want. Maybe you can come with us, just once? If you're not too busy, I mean. Abbie said you might be too busy, but that I should ask anyway and see."

I look over at Abbie, who flushes with a guilty smile. She truly is remarkable. How could I have ever doubted someone who is so clearly devoted to my family? Natasha, that's why. Natasha took full advantage of me during our relationship and left me with atrocious trust issues. And now it's on me to overcome them.

Starting now.

"As usual, Abbie is correct," I cede. "But yes, I'd love to join you. I'll take some time off to make sure I can fit it into my schedule."

"Yes!" Jude bounces in her seat and pumps her fist. "Cassie's figuring out the trail for us, so you can choose the picnic spot, Abbie."

"That sounds perfect. I think I know just the place," Abbie says. Her eyes meet mine again, eyes full of knowing.

Memories slide through me of the time we went riding and I showed her my favorite place on the estate, near a creek. That was the day I fucked her delicious ass cheeks, taking full advantage of the body that craved mine. I remember how quickly her body responded when I applied a little force around her neck, how she arched against me and begged for more.

I make a mental note to take her back to that same exact spot this weekend. The last time we were there, I didn't let her come, taking all I wanted and leaving her unsatisfied. I'll make it up to her this time, let her come long and loud in the middle of everything that is mine. Just thinking about her cries echoing off the trees makes my pants tight.

I owe Abbie that, and so much more. I plan to let her collect in full. Many times.

We pull around in the circular drive and stop outside the front door, where the full staff waits outside to greet us and unload our luggage. Esmeralda beams as we exit the car.

"Mrs. Ratliff isn't with you?" she asks innocently, taking Jude's hand.

"Mrs. Ratliff has several shows this weekend," I tell her. "It's just the three of us, I'm afraid."

"I'm sure that will do just fine," Esmeralda says.

"Let's hope so." I wink at her.

"Can I go see my horses now?" Jude begs. "Can we go riding now?"

"Not yet, love." I have business to attend to first. "I must speak with Cassie first to get things set up. Why don't you go inside and introduce Sugar Cube to the rest of your toys?"

"Ooh!" Jude beams. "She would love that, won't you, Sugar Cube? Abbie, can you help me?"

"Of course." Abbie beams right back, seeming less stressed than she's been the entire time we've been in the City.

Natasha does that to people. After I deal with Quinn, I will have control over my estate once again, and I can begin the process of disentangling Natasha from my house—permanently.

"Please take my things up to my room while I go see Miss Ko in the stables," I tell Esmeralda, unable to wait any longer. The sooner this is done, the better.

"Of course, Mr. Ratliff."

Even the air here is better, cleaner than in the city. My legs enjoy the stretch walking across the grounds, and my heart starts to beat at ease, as though my entire being had been on guard for days. Being with Natasha will do that, too. This break is going to be good for everyone.

I find Cassie in the stables, neatly braiding Desi's

mane. Jude's effect on everyone appears to be lasting, which makes me proud. My daughter, though young, is already a powerful force. She'll do great things one day.

"Mr. Ratliff!" Cassie exclaims as I walk in. "Welcome back. I didn't expect to see you so soon."

"Oh no? You aren't preparing Jude's horse for her?" I ask with a grin.

She laughs. "I wanted Desi to be ready just in case."

Cassie's always been a wonderful employee. I can't hold her personally responsible for the actions of her insubordinates, at least in this case.

"I need to talk to one of the stable hands, Quinn Dempsey," I say, as casually as I can. "Where might I find him?"

"Oh." Her brow furrows. "Quinn's actually out of town for the next few days. He's at an event in Rochester."

"Rochester?" That's at least a four- or five-hour drive west of here. I work to keep a neutral expression on my face. How convenient. Quinn must have heard we were planning to return and took his leave to hide from my wrath and retribution. But he can't hide forever.

"The livestock auction. There were some horses you wanted to acquire?" She tilts her head to the side, just a little, and continues braiding. "I figured I should be here for Jude's lessons, so I sent him in my stead. Is that okay?"

"It's perfectly fine."

"You sure?" She offers me a curious look. "Is there something I can help you with?"

"No need to fret about it, Cassie. It's a simple business matter to attend to. How has he been in the stables?"

"He's a good employee. Hard worker, mostly."

"Mostly? Has he stepped out of line?"

Cassie shrugs. "You know how the younger ones are. Sometimes they forget their place."

"Indeed. Well. As I'm sure you can imagine, Jude is eager to return to her horses. I'll be joining her and Abbie on a trail ride, as well. Can you prepare everything for us?"

"Of course, Mr. Ratliff."

Double damn that I cannot fire Quinn yet, but at least he won't be here to sour my mood with the girls. I return to the house to find Jude and Abbie in the living room. Abbie looks a little peaked, which I'm sure means that Jude has been relentless about riding.

"Daddy! Can I go ride?"

"Almost. Cassie's getting everything ready as we speak. Why don't you join her in the stables and say hello to all the horses? I need to talk to Abbie for a moment."

"Okay!" She all but dances her way out of the room while singing a song.

"She's very excited." Abbie smiles at me. "I guess we're going to spend a lot of time out of doors?"

"I don't doubt it. But first, may I speak with you in my office?"

She frowns a little. "Is everything okay?"

"Come."

A foreign emotion swells through me as I lead her across the house. Anticipation? Excitement? It's been so long. As soon as she enters the office, I shut the door behind her.

"What did you need to—"

I cut her off with my mouth. My hands slide into her hair as I pull her close to me, claiming her with all the fierce passion swelling through me. I kiss her with the triumphant exhilaration of a man who finally has exactly what he wants. Abbie responds in kind, grabbing at my clothes and pulling me closer. When I thrust my tongue against hers more aggressively, as if I'm fucking her mouth with mine, she groans and pulls back, gasping for breath.

"What was that for?" she asks, chest heaving.

"I am not good at apologies, Abbie. I don't make them often. But it doesn't escape me that I owe you one of a great magnitude." I step back to study her face, illuminated in the afternoon sun. "I told you I would make things right. That starts today."

Something in her eyes goes flinty. "You know that saying, 'Love means never having to say you're sorry'?"

"Yes..."

"Well, it's bullshit. When you hurt someone, especially someone you care about, you apologize."

I nod slowly. She's right, I know she is, but the words stick in my throat.

"You asked me to give this thing a chance," she goes on. "But how can I possibly do that when you refuse to say you're sorry?"

"Abbie—"

"I need to hear you say it! I don't care how much you hate it, I need to hear the words. Talking about apologizing isn't the same thing as doing it. It's a sign of respect, not weakness."

I frown. "I know. And I know I hurt you. Badly."

"Yes. You did."

"And..." I reach out and take both of her hands in mine, looking her in the eyes. I never thought two simple words could be so difficult to say out loud. This is even harder than my bloody wedding vows were. I take a deep breath. "And I'm sorry, Abbie. I am."

She blinks hard against the tears welling in her eyes, and something inside me loosens. I've repaired something broken just now. I hadn't realized it could feel so liberating.

"I'm sorry," I say again. "I'm sorry I didn't believe you. I'm sorry for all the times I yelled, or made you feel like you were anything less than the incredible woman you are. Abigail Montgomery, I'm s—"

I don't get to finish, as she throws herself in my arms and kisses me so hard that I stumble back against the door. She doesn't stop, though both of us are laughing now.

"You are mine, Abbie," I tell her. "And I am yours. If you can forgive this old man, my heart is in your hands."

"I'll take it," she whispers against my lips.

Our kiss grows more tender, imbued with the thrill of our reaffirmations and her forgiveness and countless unspoken things. I slip my hand up her shirt and gently cup the swells of her breasts, seeking her nipples through the fabric of her bra. She moans, digging her hips into mine, the zipper of her shorts grinding against my raging erection. She gasps and immediately fumbles for my pants.

"The horses are waiting," I murmur regretfully.

"You have time for this," she says, full of mischief. "I know how to make you come."

I kiss her harder, pulling her hair taut, and place a final kiss on her throat. Then she drops to her knees, licking her lips, my cock already in her hands.

Oh yes, I am home.

Chapter Seventeen

Graham

THE NEXT MORNING, I'm halfway through my coffee and toast, thumbing through the stack of newspapers in front of me, when I realize what I'm doing and forcefully push them away.

Turning to Jude, I tell her, "I think I'll catch up on my papers later. Let's start the day with something fun instead."

"But you always read the papers," Jude says around a mouthful of Mary's Italian baked eggs. I give her a stern look and she flushes. "Well, you do!"

"Be that as it may, I'm on holiday this weekend." I grab my napkin and lean over to wipe a string of melted cheese off her chin. Jude waves me away with a giggle. "The rest of the world can wait. I want to spend time with you."

"So you're gonna come swim with us?" she asks.

I glance over at Abbie and realize that she isn't in a robe at all, but a silky swimsuit cover-up, leaving both plenty and little to the imagination. I do enjoy her in a swimsuit.

"Isn't it a bit early?" I ask.

"Not if you're 'on holiday,'" Abbie says, raising her eyebrows with a smile. "What do you think, Daddy? You want to come play with us?"

The way Abbie says "Daddy" makes me shift in my seat. I catch Abbie's gaze and flick my eyes towards my daughter, but Jude doesn't seem to notice the sudden tension between me and Abbie over her relentless pleading.

"How can I say no to that face?" I say to Jude, pointedly ignoring Abbie's teasing grin. "But you know you have to wait thirty minutes after eating so you don't get a cramp."

"Dad." Jude gives me a stern look. "Not all swimming is in the water. Sometimes you lay out to tan. Right, Abbie?"

"Right, Judey."

"What are you teaching my child?" I ask plaintively, but my voice is light.

"All the important things," Abbie tosses back. "Someone in this house needs to know how to relax."

"I can relax!" I protest. "I'm very good at relaxing."

Abbie smirks. "Prove it."

"Very well." I feel warm from the challenge and the possibilities. "I will join you ladies at the pool today and show you just how well Daddy can relax."

I wink at Abbie and her cheeks flush. It's one of my favorite things about her, the way her body reacts so quickly to mine. Her blushes, her moans, the way her nipples always perk up when I'm around. If I stare hard enough, I can see the outline of them now through her swimsuit.

"Are you chilly, Miss Montgomery?"

Abbie glances down at her chest and clears her throat. "Only when you're around."

"Why would you be cold around Daddy?" Jude asks, looking back and forth between the pair of us. "He's not an ice monster."

"He can be," Abbie teases.

"Hey!" I hold up my hands. "I'm sitting right here."

"Enough talking!" Jude huffs. "More eating, so we can go to the pool."

"He's still working on his toast. Cut your old man some slack; he's not as quick as he used to be in his youth," Abbie admonishes with a grin.

"I am not old," I protest. I don't feel thirty-five, especially with Abbie and Jude around. I feel younger, and I know I look younger than most people my age, even with the gray at my temples. And my glasses make me look refined, not elderly. Still, I subtly slide them off and toss them on the pile of newspapers. "I'm dignified."

"That means old," Jude says matter-of-factly.

"Well then, I can see where I'm not welcome." I rise from my chair with a faux huff.

"Daddy!" Jude laughs. "Sit down! Eat!"

The rest of breakfast unfolds just like this—light-hearted and full of laughter. I can feel the stress I carry in my neck and shoulders lessening by the second. Jude looks happier than I've seen her in months, and even

Abbie seems at ease in my presence, which is new for her.

This, I think, *would be nice every day*.

The thought pulls me up short. Every day. What am I thinking? Twenty-four hours of relaxation and here I am, musing over the future? I need to shelve that.

I make Jude wait the requisite thirty minutes after breakfast before we go to the pool by distracting her with old episodes of my favorite childhood cartoon, *Count Duckula*. Jude seems rather horrified by it, but it's a delightful punch of nostalgia that sets my soul at ease.

Afterward, Jude turns to look at me quizzically, nestled under my arm on the couch. "You used to watch that?"

"All the time." I kiss the top of her head. "It was my favorite show when I was young."

"When, a hundred years ago?"

"This is my formal request to stop calling me old." I give her a squeeze. "It wasn't *that* long ago."

"Abbie." Jude turns to look at her, sitting on her other side. "Do *you* remember that show?"

"I think it's a British thing. But no. It was way before my time." Abbie grins cheekily.

"All right, I think it's pool time now. Enough piling on old dad." I pick up Jude by the waist and she squeals in glee. "Are you ready for another cannonball championship?"

"Yes!" Jude shouts and wiggles out of my grasp. "Race you to the pool!"

"Not if I race you first!" Abbie jumps up and runs out of the room. Jude squeals again and trails after her, running as fast as her short legs can pump. I trail after them at a leisurely pace, soaking up the view.

Abbie's backside is obscured by her brightly colored cover-up, but I know exactly how the curvature of her ass looks, no matter what she's wearing. And watching Jude fly across the patio, giggling and shouting at the top of her lungs, brings me great joy.

Jude jumps straight into the pool and bobs back up like a seal. "Who's going to judge?"

"I will!" Abbie volunteers, slipping her cover-up off and revealing a skimpy little string bikini. She settles into a lounger and drops a pair of large sunglasses over her eyes. "We'll see which Ratliff reigns supreme."

"I don't think so." I scoop Abbie up and hold her like a baby in my arms, walking toward the edge of the pool. She lets out a small squeal.

"Put me down! What are you doing?"

"Everyone needs to play." I hoist her higher, trying to dislodge her arms from around my neck so I can throw her in. "That means you, too."

"But someone needs to judge!" Abbie protests. "Jude! Tell him!"

"What do you think, Judebug?" I jiggle Abbie in my arms. "Should I throw her in?"

"No!" Abbie wails.

"Yes!" Jude claps her hands. "Throw her! Throw her! Throw her!"

"Graham Ratliff." Abbie is stern but she can't keep the laugh from her voice. "You put me down right now."

I grin mischievously. "As you wish."

I jump into the pool, taking Abbie in with me. I can

hear Jude cracking up when we break the surface, and Abbie paddles away in a hurry and splashes me in the face.

"So rude!" she says, pushing wet hair out of her eyes.

"You're welcome." I wink at her. "Now, how are we going to judge this competition?"

"I'll be the judge this time," Jude proclaims, climbing out of the pool. "After I go first." The cheeky little monkey takes off running and cannonballs right next to us, sending a huge splash to cover Abbie and me.

"All right, old man." Abbie climbs out of the pool and then makes a show of readjusting her suit bottoms, drawing my attention to her ripe, round ass. "I'll go first."

"Ladies should always go first," I tell her.

She mock-curtsies, then breaks into a gymnast-style run before hurling herself into the pool. A modest splash breaks the edge of the pool and gets Jude wet, who giggles and cheers.

"Seven!" she declares.

"A seven?!" Abbie gapes at her. "Oh, come on! That was at least an eight."

"Jude was generous. I would have given it a six," I say with a shrug.

"Is that right?" Abbie splashes me again. "Okay, Mr. Hot Shot, let's see what you've got."

"Charmed." I shoot back and hop out of the pool.

Is this what relaxation looks like? Warm pool mornings and competitions with my giggling child and blushing woman? Not stressing about the press or the papers, not worrying about the Devil in Heels? I would do this every day if I could.

I start further back than either of the girls, and run hard to the pool. My feet clear the edge and I go soaring into the air, clasp my arms around my knees, and drop like a stone into the water. I can feel pool water suck in around me as I do, and when I break the surface, I'm delighted to see I've sufficiently soaked both Jude and Abbie with my masterful cannonball.

"Wow, Daddy!" Jude wipes her hair from her face, cheeks stretched under a smile. "That was amazing!"

"It was all right," Abbie concedes, smoothing her hair back over her head in a way that makes me want to grab a fistful of it and push her to her knees. "Could have been better."

"Better?" I scoff. "Half the bloody pool jumped out! What say you, honorable judge?"

"Ten!" She claps. "Winner, winner!"

I bow grandly in the shallow end, laughing with them both. And that's how we spend the rest of our morning. Jude organizes several pool races and more cannonball competitions. Abbie kicks my ass in the relay race, but I am the undisputed cannonball champion. Perhaps I should have a trophy made up to celebrate. We're all lazing about on lounge chairs when Mary pops her head out the back door.

"Lunchtime!" she chirps, bringing out a picnic basket to the covered patio. She spreads a checkered cloth over the table and lays out a tray of croissant sandwiches, cut up fruits and vegetables, assorted cold salads, and a pitcher of lemonade.

"This looks like a fantastic spread," I tell Mary,

helping to set out the plates, cutlery, and napkins. "Thank you so much."

Jude cheers and rushes over, loading up her plate with a sandwich, some macaroni salad, a pile of red grapes, and a handful of carrot sticks. Then she plops into a chair, pops a grape into her mouth, and swings her legs as she chews. For a moment, she almost looks like she's four again. Four and unbothered by anything the world has to throw at her.

This is what I've been missing. I only need look at my child to understand what has to happen in my life, how to move forward. The question is, how can I with Natasha in the way?

Abbie places a hand on my shoulder, and I turn to see a look of concern on her face.

"You okay?"

"Yes. Of course." I shake the thoughts away and offer a smile. "Loads better than I've been recently. Just thinking."

"I think you do that too much."

"What, think?"

"Overthink."

Well. She's not wrong. I'd say a large part of my success was the result of flagrant overthinking and over-planning, always being two steps ahead of my competitors at any given moment. "You may be on to something there," I admit.

"I know." Abbie grins and picks up a sandwich. "But it's nice seeing you out here with your critical analytical side shut off. It's fun."

"I told you I could be fun."

She gently nudges me with her shoulder and drops into a chair next to Jude, who starts animatedly rehashing our morning in the pool. I don't think I've ever seen her happier. I stand there a moment longer, savoring my lemonade, just soaking it all in.

This is what a family should be.

Chapter Eighteen

Abbie

AFTER SEVERAL HOURS in the pool and a late afternoon trail ride, I don't even need to put Jude to sleep—because when Graham and I go to tuck her in, we find her snoring softly, her copy of *Black Beauty* facedown on her chest.

With a smile, Graham gently pulls the book away and replaces it with one of Jude's stuffed horses. The way he strokes her hair and kisses her temple gives me a rush of warmth inside, despite the fact that Jude isn't even my kid.

What is it about men and their ability to be good dads? It's like we see them at their most gentle, most caring, most vulnerable, and that makes them sexier than ever. I want to bang his mother loving brains out.

We tiptoe out of the room, holding hands.

"Do you have any plans this evening, Miss Montgomery?" Graham asks as he runs a finger down my throat, and between that and his clipped accent, my panties are about to burn right off.

"I was thinking about washing my hair," I tease. "What about you, Mr. Ratliff?"

"Please, call me Graham." He grins, and in the dim lights, he looks positively irresistible. I can't stop myself from lifting onto my tiptoes and kissing him softly on the lips.

"Oh," he murmurs, surprised. "And to what do I owe this pleasure?"

"These lights make you look good."

"Don't be silly. I look good in any light."

"God, you're cocky. It's so unbecoming," I whisper, pressing myself into him to steal another kiss.

"Stick with me and you'll be coming, too," he says huskily.

I stifle a laugh. "Fine, I'll bite. What did you have in mind for tonight?"

"It's a surprise."

"Oh really? I do love surprises."

Graham kisses me one last time and then walks away, holding up his arm and pointing at his watch. "Twenty minutes. I suggest you wear pants."

Ooh, I wonder what he's up to. I hurry to my room to brush out the mess that my riding helmet made of my hair and give my teeth a quick brush. Then I change into jeans and freshen up my makeup, with a generous coat of Teenage Fantasy. Because I know what this man likes.

A few pinches to my cheeks later, I feel complete. I feel...beautiful. And I am so ready to see what Graham has in store for the evening.

Downstairs, I find Graham sitting on the steps, thumbs flying across his phone. He turns at the sound of my footsteps and a smile blooms across his face, so warm that I can feel my own cheeks heating instantly, butterflies assaulting me from head to toe.

"You're stunning." He holds out his hand for me and walks me the rest of the way down the stairs, as if I'm in a ballgown and not just jeans and a T-shirt.

"Stop it," I smile. At the bottom, I do a little twirl under his arm.

"*Truly* stunning, Abbie." He dips me like an old-fashioned movie star.

"Stop it some more." I try not to giggle, but he's got me all up in my feelings right now. This side of Graham is so rare, but so amazing. I wish he could stay this way forever.

"Are you ready for your surprise?" he asks.

"More than."

Graham leans in to kiss me again and I lose myself in him, savoring the softness of his lips and the instant rush of heat between my legs.

"I hope you're ready for more horses," he murmurs.

I pout. "My thighs are so sore. We already did so much riding today."

"I promise it won't be far. Come now, you need to work out those thigh muscles." He winks at me and I melt.

"Fine, but I'm going to complain the whole way there."

"I wouldn't expect anything less."

Out front, two horses are waiting for us. I don't actually complain at all, because Graham has me cracking up the entire time. He cracks jokes and tells more wild stories about his days on his grandmother's farm. Picturing him as a rebellious and scrappy ten-year-old boy is one of the funniest things I can imagine.

Both fortunately and unfortunately, we stop riding all too soon. He's brought me to a familiar tree in the woods, only this time it's decked out in string lights to produce a beautiful glow. Under the canopy of branches is a checkered picnic blanket and a bottle of champagne and some kind of thick glass dome. As we get closer, I realize it's covering what looks like a decadent but perfectly small chocolate cake. Chocolate cake!

"Graham," I gasp. "This is incredible."

"Come." He takes my hand and leads me to the blanket. Then he turns on a Bluetooth speaker and taps at his phone screen until suddenly, Etta James's smooth voice croons at us amidst the magic of the forest at nighttime. "May I have this dance?"

I stare at him open-mouthed as I let him pull me into his arms. "Who is this Graham and what did you do with the old one?" I ask as we sway under the golden lights.

"This is what you'd call *Holiday Graham*."

I giggle, giddy and love drunk. "Well, I like him. Tell him to stick around."

"I'll be sure to relay the message to old Graham, so I can have you entirely to myself," he growls against my ear and my whole body shudders.

We slowly dance to the music, our heads pressed together. I feel like I'm floating. I don't know what brought on Holiday Graham, but I think I'm in love with him. Seeing who Graham can be when he wants to be is intoxicating. He cups my ass through my jeans and presses me against him, his hardness rubbing against my center.

"I didn't know you liked to dance," I say softly.

He pushes me away for a small twirl and pulls me back in. "I'm full of surprises. I thought you liked surprises."

"I do."

Graham gently bites my lower lip. "Good. Because that's what I'm here for."

Ooh-*la-la*. Our eyes meet and I try to imprint this moment into my memory, of the two of us holding each other right now, surrounded by twinkling lights. Joined together in the place where I first felt the power of his manhood. Where I learned I liked it rough under his hands. I want to remember this version of Graham who is gazing down at me with something like adoration in his eyes, kissing me like I'm the only person in the world.

Graham dips his head down to bite my shoulder and places a kiss on my neck. I shiver and pull his mouth to mine. The way our lips collide is electric. Then he pulls me in for a spin and dip as we dance some more.

"Thank you for giving me another chance," he murmurs into my hair.

"You're welcome."

He shakes his head. "I was a bloody twat, Abbie. And I'm sorry for that."

I pull back and cup his cheek. "All is forgiven. Your last apology was enough."

"Don't." Graham lets out a breath. "Don't just say you forgive me because you feel it's the right thing to do. I hurt you terribly and I've got a long road ahead of me making it up to you. But I will, because it's important to me. You and I are important to me. Do you understand?"

I melt. "I do. Do I wish things had gone differently? Yes, of course. I wish that story had never gone public. I wish our reputations hadn't taken a hit like that, especially considering where we're at in our individual lives. God. But I can also understand why you reacted the way you did. You were under attack, and you had no idea where it was coming from. So you lashed out. I can only imagine how far you'd go to protect your reputation, your business—"

"It's not just my reputation, it's my family," he says passionately. "It's Jude. Everything in my life, it's always for Jude. But I didn't have to be so cruel to you."

He looks away, and I know this is hard for him, exposing himself like this and speaking from his heart—which makes it that much easier to forgive. I take his chin and turn his face toward me with a playful smile, trying to lighten the load he's carrying. "So how do you plan to make it up to me?"

"I thought you'd never ask."

As he kisses me, his hands slide under my T-shirt, and he gives a murmur of surprise when his fingers brush my nipples instead of my bra. "Naughty girl."

"That's how you like it."

"That's how *you* like it."

"Shut up and kiss me, Ratliff."

He obliges, running his thumbs across my pert nipples, stirring the heat of want that's throbbing in my lower belly. Then in one fluid motion, he pulls my shirt up over my head and dips his mouth to lavish my nipples with his tongue, hot and fierce. I moan against him and tug at his shirt. He pauses long enough to pull it off for me and then returns to sucking on my nipples. The feel of our bare skin ignites the flames in my veins. It feels so perfect, so right.

We lower ourselves onto the blanket and our kisses deepen as we shed the rest of our clothing. I tilt my head back and close my eyes as Graham trails kisses down my chest and belly, until he's perched between my legs. When he gently pushes my thighs wide apart, my adrenaline surges, my heart racing faster. I reach down and lace my fingers into his hair, trying to relax.

"Eat me," I moan.

"I thought you'd never ask," Graham teases.

He blows gently on my lips before parting them with his tongue, and then the heavens open as his mouth moves upward to make love to my swollen nub. My body arches with every hypnotic flick and drag of his tongue, euphoria making my vision blurry. It is the most divine experience of my life. I writhe under him as his tongue swirls over me, the pressure building into something beautiful and intoxicating. My heavy breathing gives way to a crescendo of moans, my toes curling with pleasure.

I'm about to reach the point of no return when Graham suddenly pushes himself up and kisses his way back to me, leaving the taste of me on my tongue. He rubs his cock against my soaked slit, just enough to tease me but not enough to satisfy my longing for him.

"Gimme," I breathe.

"Oh, is this what you want? I rather thought you enjoyed my fine work a minute ago."

"Not good enough." I pout. "I want you inside me. Now."

He chuckles deeply and rolls onto his back, pulling me on top of him. I reach down and feed his cock into me, inch by delicious inch, both of us breathing hard at the feel of our connection. Then I start to rock back and forth, fucking him hard, already so turned on by the way he ate my pussy that I can't stop myself from riding him like a wild woman.

"More," I grind out. "More, more, more."

His hands come up to pull my face back down to his, and all I can see and smell and taste is Graham. His thrusts match mine, in time to the music, his hips rolling. I straighten up and then lean back with my legs spread wide, angling my hips so I can feel his girth filling me completely. My tits bounce with every stroke, my moans turning to desperate cries.

"Fuck yes," Graham pants.

He reaches up and wraps a hand around my throat, gently pressing his fingers into the side of my neck, gradually increasing his grip with each thrust until I'm gasping.

"Is it too much?" he asks, easing up.

"No. Never."

I cover his hand with mine, forcing his fingers tighter again, feeling drunk under the lights. My climax builds with every pump of his cock, with every bounce, every breath.

"*Graham*," I moan.

When he pulls me down by my throat to kiss me again, my entire world lights up as an orgasm rips through me. I let my wails echo off the trees while Graham growls in my ear about how hot it is when I come, and not a minute later he's unleashing his own groans into the night air.

Oh yes, all is forgiven.

Chapter Nineteen

Graham

"Ronaldo's driving us into town to catch the new Pixar movie at the cineplex," Abbie tells me, poking her head into my office. "Want to join us? We're getting ice cream afterward."

"I'd love to. But it'll have to wait until next time," I say regretfully.

I'd rather spend the afternoon with them than deal with what business needs tending, but I'd be lying if I said I wasn't also looking forward to this bit of nastiness. In fact, I extended our trip here an extra few days just so I wouldn't miss it.

"I have a meeting that I can't move," I add.

"Really? What happened to Holiday Graham?" Abbie teases. "I thought you were taking some time off."

I spread my hands. "Holiday Graham can only be here if Business Graham attends to things every now and again."

"Who's Holiday Graham?" Jude asks, popping out

from behind Abbie. "Does that mean we're going somewhere?"

"No, no trips." I miss the days when I could pick my daughter up and swing her onto my shoulders. I think about trying it now, but decide my back doesn't need the pain. "It's just what Abbie calls me when I relax. And I am relaxed; I just need to take care of a few things today."

"Aww!" Jude whines. "But we're supposed to be hanging out together!"

"I know, I know. And we will." I get up and cross the room to kiss the top of her head. "But why don't you and Abbie enjoy your movie date, and by the time you get back, I'll be ready to play again. I promise."

"So you'll go swimming with us later?" she asks, crossing her arms.

I nod. "Yes. *After* I take care of things. I solemnly swear."

Jude studies me for a moment and I put on my best face of innocence. She finally seems satisfied. "Fine. But you better not be lying."

"I'm not. Cross my heart. Maybe you can bring me back a double scoop of mint chocolate chip while you're at it."

"I'll see what I can do," Jude says seriously. Behind her, Abbie grins.

"Come on, kiddo," she says, gently taking Jude's shoulder. "The sooner we get to our date, the sooner we can come home and get to cannonballing."

"Okay. Bye, Daddy!" With that, Jude zips down the hall.

"See you soon," I call after her retreating figure.

"Bye, Daddy," Abbie whispers, slowly tracing her finger down the fly of my pants and flashing me a wicked smile before she leaves to catch up to Jude.

As soon as I hear the front door slam, I make my way to the stables to find Cassie. She's not with any of the horses, so I go around the building to where the office is located.

"Hey, Mr. Ratliff." Cassie looks up from the computer at the small desk and slips a pair of glasses on top of her head. "To what do I owe this pleasure?"

"Has Quinn Dempsey returned?"

"Yes, sir. Just this morning. He should be back any minute from a hay run."

"Excellent. When he gets back, send him to my office up at the house."

"Sure thing." Cassie nods. "Anything else I can do for you?"

"Start looking for his replacement. And I'd appreciate it if you could pack up his things."

She stiffens, looking concerned. "Is there something I need to be made aware of, sir? So I can...better move forward in the future? I didn't hire him myself, but I am his supervisor, so—"

"No, that won't be necessary. You're doing a perfect job. It's nothing to worry about."

I nod my farewell and head to my office to pour a whiskey. I'll need all my wits about me if I'm not to strangle this vile little ingrate, and that means having a drink to steady my hand.

I sit at my desk in my office, reviewing a portfolio of investments for one of the bank's wealthier clients, but all

I can think about is Abbie. I can still taste her on my tongue, mixing with the sweet smokiness of the whiskey. Last night, we danced and made love under the trees, and then I fed her chocolate ganache cake and champagne, and then we made love again, this time in a clearing under the stars, talking afterward until we were almost too tired to return to the house. After a quick, hot shower, we spent the night in each other's arms. It was a perfect evening. I'm fairly certain my apology was well-received.

And now, I'm finally going to be able to eliminate the cockroach who tried to invade my home and destroy my relationship. Everything will be right as rain.

I stop at one whiskey and am about to check the time again when heavy bootsteps echo off the marble in the hall outside my office. Enter one Quinn Dempsey. He's positively ordinary: early-20s, blond hair, blue eyes, a slightly thick neck and some fledgling muscles under his rolled shirtsleeves. He isn't bad looking, but he isn't all that interesting either. He's mundane. Oozing unwarranted self-confidence, but still wet behind the ears.

I have to stop myself from laughing out loud at my former jealousy when this boy took Abbie out on a date. My jealousy stemmed from wanting to keep Abbie to myself, but the fact that I allowed myself to forget who I am over this pathetic pup is humorous.

"You wanted to see me, Mr. Ratliff?" he says.

He looks out of place in my ornate office wearing his work clothes. He stands uncomfortably, like he knows he doesn't belong here. And he's right.

"I did."

Leaning against the doorframe, he glances around.

"This is nice. I've never been in here before."

"There was never a reason before," I say coldly. "Have a seat."

His whole body seems to tense at my tone. "I'd rather stand."

"And I'd rather sprout wings, but I'm woefully grounded. *Sit.*" I cast a stern look and Quinn reluctantly obeys. "Now. Cassie tells me you were recently in Rochester for livestock acquisition."

"Yes, I was." Quinn sits up straighter, as though he feels safer now that we're in familiar territory. "It went well. I gave my report to Cassie, but I'm happy to discuss it with you."

"Is that right?" I recline in my chair and steeple my fingers. "That's all you were doing?"

Quinn looks confused. "Sir? I'm not sure I understand."

"Perhaps you'll understand this, then."

I withdraw the manila envelope from my desk drawer that Bowen gave me, full of evidence pertaining to the recent press leak. Slowly, I pull out each photo and report and signed affidavit, letting each document settle on the desktop before pulling out the next.

Copies of emails and cell phone records. *Boom.*

Photos of him meeting with reporters. *Boom.*

A deposit statement showing multiple influxes of cash appearing in Quinn's personal checking account. *Boom.*

Piece after piece of incriminating evidence comes out, and with each piece, Quinn grows paler. When I'm finished, I recline in my chair and stare him down. "You weren't using this trip as a cover to spread your story further?"

To his credit, he doesn't flinch. "I'm not sure what you're implying, but—"

"There's no need to 'imply' anything, Mr. Dempsey. Your actions have been made perfectly clear." I gesture to the photos. "You concocted a story about myself and my nanny, and you sold it. The evidence is all here."

His gaze goes hard. "You can't prove that I did anything."

"Are you joking? That's exactly what this is." I slam my fist on the pile on the desk. "Are you really that daft? I have photographic evidence, bank statements, admissions from reporters. All of them point to you and you alone. Are you daring to tell me this is all fabricated?"

"Yes." His poker face begins to crack. I can see the sweat beading at his hairline.

"Do you know what I do to people who fuck me over, Quinn?" I lean forward, steepling my fingers like some comic book villain. "Do you have any *idea* what I'm capable of?"

"Not capable of keeping your personal business private, it appears," he has the audacity to say.

Anger roils through me, and I stand up so fast my chair almost upends. "You are walking a dangerous line here, Dempsey. It's not looking good for you."

He has nothing to say and breaks eye contact first.

"You framed Abbie and attempted to soil her reputation in a pathetic attempt to get me out of the picture, leave her vulnerable and reviled, and win over her affections," I continue. "Why, Quinn? Did you want revenge after she rejected you? Or are you simply the kind of predator who needs to weaken his prey before going in for the kill?"

A slow smile spreads across his face and he lifts his head to look me dead in the eye again. "You've got it all wrong. I don't need to fuck *the help*."

"Is that right?"

He reclines back in his chair, hands behind his head, bizarrely at ease. "I didn't frame Abbie to try to get her back. I know she's so far up your ass she can't see the light of day."

"Blackmail, then?"

"You're a little slow on the uptake, aren't you?" Quinn says nastily, sounding pleased with himself. "I'll spell it out, then. I don't need to fuck *the help* because I'm fucking *your wife*."

Realization suddenly dawns on me. "Excuse me?"

"You heard me." He has a sickeningly smug look on his face. "I'm fucking Natasha! And she is a goddamn *tiger* in bed. Why would I want your worthless nanny?"

"You will not insult the members of my staff," I say through gritted teeth.

"You mean your lover?" He laughs. "It's not exactly a state secret. Everyone sees the way you two act."

The urge to rip off his head hums through my veins, my hands clenching at my sides. I think about doing it, about leaping over the desk and punching him until his face is nothing more than a bloody pulp. I think about the hell I put Abbie through, all because of this fucking bellend.

"So Natasha put you up to it," I say. It's all making

sense now.

"She didn't need to," Quinn says, but he's obviously lying.

I laugh. "Dear God. You sorry sod, you can't even see how far in it you are. Natasha won't be keeping you around once she's done with you. You're a fucking stable boy. Or are you completely ignorant to her track record of using people and then throwing them away once they've served their purpose? She's a bloodsucker. A locust. A fucking succubus."

Quinn shrugs, but I can tell I've gotten to him. "I guess we'll see about that."

"I guess we shall. But let me remind you of something, Mr. Dempsey. Every member of my staff signs a Nondisclosure Agreement with their employment paperwork, with strict stipulations that they do not discuss the goings-on in my house. Here is a copy of yours, in case your memory isn't serving you."

Dropping into my chair, I produce another paper from the envelope and slide it over to him.

"Your actions are in direct violation of your employment contract. Not only is your ass fired, effective immediately, but you are also being sued."

This gets his attention. "You can't sue me for this."

"Oh, I absolutely can. Slander. Libel. Violation of contract. Defamation, sexual harassment, and I'm unsure if Abbie will be seeking damages for the psychological and emotional distress she's experienced, but I imagine that could become quite costly."

Quinn stands, his face pale. "I'm leaving."

"That is an excellent idea. But first, there's someone I

need you to meet. Bow?"

From the hallway, my attorney walks in holding a briefcase, a file folder tucked under her arm. She smiles, and it's the scary kind. "Quinn Dempsey, you are hereby officially served."

"What?" His face goes ashen. "You can't do this!"

"I can and I have," I tell him. "Cassie has already boxed up your personal effects. You will collect them from the stables and then go. I'll be seeing you in court soon, Mr. Dempsey."

"But—" Quinn stammers.

"If you don't mind, Mr. Dempsey, I believe you're occupying the space between myself and a very good whiskey, and that is not a place you want to be," Bowen says good-naturedly, dropping the file with her hundred-plus-page lawsuit in his lap. "So if you'll just step aside."

I reach for my decanter and a fresh glass for Elise. "You got here at the most opportune time, Bow. And Mr. Dempsey, I really must suggest you fuck directly off before I have to report you to the police for trespassing. You don't want to add more to your legal troubles."

Quinn stands, his legs trembling, Bow's thick file in one hand. "This isn't over."

"Quite the contrary, this is precisely over." I pour out two celebratory whiskeys and slide Bow's glass across the desk toward her. "Now get the hell out of my house. I've an appointment with an old friend."

Trembling with rage, Quinn takes off, slamming the door behind him.

Bow and I clink glasses in a toast and then drink.

Firing someone has never been more satisfying.

Chapter Twenty

Abbie

RONALDO IS DRIVING us back to the Upper West Side, and Jude is slumped silently in her seat, acting as sullen as I feel. She just had her Spanish lesson using the video-conferencing app on Graham's laptop, and she's now officially missing her riding instruction with Cassie—and her time with Desi. I don't have to be a detective to guess what's going on in her pretty little head.

I can't blame her for being pouty. Natasha's apartment is hell. It's suffocating and heavy with tension—whenever she's around, we all have to walk on eggshells—and everything about it screams Natasha Ratliff Lives Here. Graham can bury himself in work and business meetings, of course, but I've seen the negative impact on Jude up close and personal. When she's in NYC, she's constantly worried about her mother's mood and her parents' strained relationship, not to mention the anxiety of being so far from her horses. And yes, I obviously have my own reasons for feeling so uncomfortable and unhappy there. In the Hudson Valley, Graham and I have the freedom to be ourselves, but we have to keep everything under wraps when we're in New York.

I hate it.

On top of that, I'm beyond exhausted. Last night, Graham and I stayed up way too late having sex, and then stayed up even later talking, including about our upcoming trip back to Natasha. He apologized for putting me in her line of fire, and I almost told him about her slapping me. But ultimately, I decided to leave that one in my pocket for later. I don't want him stressing about her suspicions, or wondering what I said or did to make her get physical with me. Obviously I didn't deserve to get hit, but in hindsight, I'm not exactly proud of how I conducted myself.

"Why couldn't we just stay?" Jude murmurs plaintively, gazing sadly out the window at the increasing traffic.

"We've talked about this." Graham's voice is short and clipped, and I can tell by the expression on his face that his armor is back on. Holiday Graham is gone. Apparently packed away with the rest of the luggage this morning. "We are going back to support your mother."

"But Mommy didn't need us before. Why does she need us now?"

I turn to look at Graham, wondering how he'll spin his response. He looks like he's struggling to come up with an answer (not that I expect him to make any mention of the media frenzy surrounding our alleged affair), but Jude never stops watching him, so he sighs and finally manages, "She's been having a rough time lately."

"That's not new," Jude mutters. "Desi is going to be so mad at me for leaving again."

"I'm sure that's not true," I say soothingly. "Besides, you'll be back to ride her again soon." Judging by Graham's face, I've overstepped a bit, but I go on. "Maybe we can keep coming back on the weekends. Or plan a special day during the week when everyone is busy working. Don't worry, the horses won't even know you're gone."

"They'll know. They miss me." She glares at her dad. "And you're taking me away."

"Jude," Graham warns.

"I liked Holiday Daddy a lot better than this one. My summer vacation is ruined," she whines.

"That is *enough*. I don't want to hear another word." Graham's voice is like ice. "When we get to the apartment, you'll go straight to your room and stay there until dinner."

Jude's chin quavers, but she holds back her tears and pulls her gigantic stuffed horse tightly to her chest. "Fine! I don't want to be around you, anyway."

I press my lips together to keep from interfering and watch, eyes wide. This is very unlike Jude, and also very unlike the relaxed, jovial version of Graham that she and I have been with the last few days. It's awful to hear him snapping at her like this, but I can't imagine how much worse it must be for Jude to see him revert to jerk mode, to be the stern parent all over again.

He has to be feeling guilty about dragging us all back to New York City, but also helpless to defy Natasha's wishes, at least until the media frenzy calms down enough for him to get away from her without it looking incriminating. Maybe this bad publicity is taking more out of him and his business than I realized. How is this all affecting the bank's bottom line? Is he worried about his livelihood going under? God, and knowing that he's spent his whole life building this empire...even if it was just to prove something to himself or to the world at first, his life is all about Jude now. He's said as much himself. If he doesn't play his cards right, he could lose everything, including custody of his daughter. I wouldn't want to be in his shoes for anything.

No wonder he's acting like such a shit.

We arrive at the apartment to find Natasha gone, as expected. She usually doesn't get home until 2 or 3 a.m. on show nights, so at least we have some peace and quiet for now.

"What happened?" Graham asks me after Jude slams her bedroom door shut loud enough for us to hear it across the apartment. He looks bewildered. "How did that go sour so quickly?"

I try to choose my words carefully. "You two are building something great, but it's...it's still fragile. I know you're going through a lot at the moment, and I get it, but...I feel like you might be taking it out on Jude a little bit. Maybe you can try to keep her separate from—"

"You don't know what you're talking about. You know *nothing* of parenting, and you can't imagine the pressure I'm under thanks to this fucking public relations scandal."

Yep. Old Graham has returned, all right. So much for my effort to be tactful.

As he paws through Natasha's liquor cabinet, I sink onto a chair nearby and try to collect my thoughts. When he finally has a drink in his hand, I take a breath and look him in the eye.

"Listen. We didn't ask to be pawns in your feud with Natasha—"

"Abbie—"

"Let me finish! And you're right, I may not know about parenting *per se*, but I do know a hell of a lot about that little girl who's locked in her room right now. She just wants you to spend time with her and show her that you love her. This last week and a half was a total dream come true for Jude, and she wants that from you all the time. Having it ripped away probably feels like a slap in the face, so can you blame her for acting out?"

I'm breathing hard, totally worked up with a combination of sympathy—no, empathy—for Jude and anger on her behalf. And my own.

Graham takes a long drink and then shakes his head. "I can't give her that kind of time and attention every single day. I have responsibilities. I have work. The real world doesn't wait, Abbie. That's why people take bloody holidays in the first place." He sets his glass down on a side table with a clunk. "I can't fuck off every day to follow the whims of an eight-year-old."

"I'm not saying you have to do that. But Graham, she's a *child*. And she's been without you and her mother for so long, under the care of non-family members like me for so long, that she's just...desperate for your attention. Desperate to know she matters, that she's loved. You can be pissed at me for saying so, but I'm going to say it: she's *hurting*. You've both hurt her."

Graham stays quiet as he stares out the window, brooding. I can't tell if he's actually thinking over everything I've just said or simply trying not to lash out at me for my impertinence. Just as I'm about to get up and go check on Jude, he turns to face me again.

"Jude's changed this summer. For the better. Or I suppose, she's turned more into her old self than I've seen in ages. She laughs, she plays, she...talks. Incessantly. She's downright *bubbly* at times. I'd do anything to keep her that way, but I can't be her nanny. I have...limitations. So tell me. How do I do it? How did you do it?"

The first thing that comes to mind is more scolding on my part, more reminders of where he's consistently fallen short or disappointed Jude—but I'm not the kind to kick someone when they're down, and it's miraculous enough that he's actually listening to me. The last thing I want is for him to get all defensive and prickly again. I have to tread lightly.

"It took patience. And effort." I move as close to the edge of my seat as I can, and the only reason I don't just climb over the coffee table and into his lap is because Natasha's staff could walk through the door at any moment. "We've spent a *lot* of time together, but she still had to warm up to me. It took all summer for us to get where we are now. But I didn't push. I let her take the lead. I stuck by her side and I was kind and I waited for her to open up, and she did.

"I listened when she talked, I was enthusiastic about anything she seemed to light up about. She loves horses, I spent time with her in the stables. She wanted to braid manes, I helped her choose the ribbons. We swam almost every day because she loves that, too. I treat her like she's worthy of my time, Graham, and so should you. It's just... time. Attention and time."

His face softens for a moment, and then the hardness sets back in. "She must understand I cannot spend all day with her like you do. My job pulls me elsewhere."

"You're not wrong," I say delicately. "But she's only eight. And you work such long hours, and often you're at home but she can't even stop in and say hello. It's hard for her."

"That's no excuse for her attitude."

"Jesus, Graham. Don't do this, please. You were a kid too, once. You must know how it is, idolizing your parents and craving their attention and love and...and validation. If you keep pushing her away, you're going to destroy her sense of self-worth. You're going to lose her."

"That might have been your experience, but that doesn't mean it will be hers." His voice is harsh and it stings.

I frown at him, trying to shove my frustration away. "You know what? You're right. I had a dad who didn't spend a lot of time with me when I was a kid, and when he was finally ready to have a relationship, we had a lot of issues. But that's not why I'm telling you this—"

"Jude is not you. I am not Ford." Graham stands, pushing his chair back as he does. "Excuse me, but I have some accounts to review."

My mouth falls open. "Seriously? I hit a nerve and you're just going to walk away?"

"I'll see you at dinner." He leaves the room without another word.

Frustrated, I let out a little growl. He can't push us away like this, not after everything. He was so sincere, so apologetic, but with his stone walls up again, we'll never be able to crack him.

I go check on Jude, who is laying forlornly on her bed, tucked under a blanket with her stuffed horse, Sugar Cube. Her lashes are wet with tears and she doesn't move when I come in.

"Are you going to be okay?" I ask, dropping onto the bed to brush her hair out of her face.

Jude says nothing.

"I know it might not seem like it, but I think your dad is having a hard time being here, too," I say gently. "I think he's trying to do the right thing and help your mom, but he wishes he could still be up at the estate, and it's making him a little grumpy."

"Then why didn't we just stay there?" Jude asks. "He's the boss; people have to listen to him when he talks. Why doesn't he just tell everyone that we're going back, and that's that?"

"I don't know," I admit, and then mentally prepare myself for what I'm about to say next. "Maybe he really wants you to be able to spend time with your mom. She has to be here in the city every day when she's performing, you know?"

"My mom doesn't care if I'm here," Jude says softly. "She's barely home anyway."

"Of course she cares. She loves you. Your parents both love you. But they also work really, really hard. And that means they have crazy busy schedules. Which sucks."

"You're not supposed to say that word," she reminds me.

I shrug. "It's a bummer, then. A sucky bummer."

That gets a little smile out of her. "A sucky bummer," she agrees.

"Yeah. There's no other word for it, and I'm sorry. I know you miss them. They miss you, too. In fact, your dad was just talking to me about it. He wishes he could be with you all the time, but he can't. That whole running a bank thing, you know? It takes a lot out of him. And he wants to hang out with you more, and he can't, and that's why he got so frustrated earlier. But he told me he wants to do better. And he's going to try."

"Really? For real?"

"For real. Both of your parents care so much about you, Jude. I promise that's the truth. It may not always feel like it, but they do."

I lean in to give her a hug. Tears trickle down Jude's face. I gently wipe them away and then stroke her hair until the tears stop, hoping against hope that I haven't just lied to her.

Chapter Twenty-One

Abbie

AFTER I LEAVE JUDE, I go to the guest room that's now officially my residence at Casa Natasha and text Amanda so I can properly vent about being stuck here again.

Maybe you should just QUIT already and come stay with MEEE, she texts. *There's still a few weekends left of summer break, and now I know which clubs the delicious boys hang out at...*

I sigh and write back, *I wish I could, but I'm trying to enjoy every last second I have with Graham and Jude.*

So it's not just Mr. British Accent. You really love the kid too, huh? she texts, adding a tearful cat face emoji.

I do. I send a photo I took on the drive down here, with Jude clinging tight to her massive stuffed horse and staring forlornly out the car window like she's a montage of cross-country road tripping after a bad breakup. She's one single tear away from winning an Oscar.

UGH I'm dead, she's so cute it's ridiculous, Amanda responds. *How can I possibly be jealous of that face? Give her an extra squeeze for me. I'm sure she needs u more than I do rn.*

Before I have a chance to write back again, Graham knocks on my door to inform me that Natasha is home from her matinee performance and that we're apparently running late to a dinner reservation she made.

"I'm supposed to go, too? Or did you just want me to get Jude ready?" I ask dubiously.

He clears his throat, having the decency to look a little embarrassed for once. "Natasha has made it clear that your assistance is required. It's not entirely a...child-friendly restaurant."

"It's not a strip club, right?" I joke.

"Worse," he says dryly. "It has three Michelin stars."

"Oof. Gotcha. We'll be ready in fifteen," I tell him.

I assume that we're going out to be seen, not necessarily to enjoy ourselves, so I dress myself and Jude in classy but subdued navy blue outfits, which seems appropriate for an upscale restaurant where children (and nannies, I'm sure) are meant to blend into the woodwork. As a compromise, I let Jude pick out her own socks—rainbow striped knee-highs—and shoes, which of course end up being her riding boots. They're in fine shape, the brass buckles gleaming and the brown leather polished, not a speck of dirt to be seen, so I figure they're perfectly acceptable.

When we get to the living room, we find Natasha impatiently pacing as she waits for us, done up like a queen with her usual mountain of gold jewelry and a sequined minidress with a long, luxuriously wrinkled cream linen jacket over it. She makes an elaborate show

190

of hugging Jude, who perks up at the presence of her mother.

As much as I dislike Natasha, I know she's important to Jude—which is why it's so infuriating to me that the woman can't put in this kind of effort more often. If our last visit here was anything to go by, Natasha probably won't be seeing Jude much for the rest of the week, when the show will be putting on late performances. Because rather than coming home after the final curtain, Natasha will go out to bars and clubs and attend after-parties with other actors and celebrities, stumbling home under the influence of God knows what just before sunrise. Jude will receive a pat on the head in passing when a hungover Natasha leaves for the play later that afternoon, and if Graham isn't at a meeting, he'll receive a nasty comment or a glare.

I don't understand why Natasha insists on keeping them close in the first place. Are Jude and Graham like trophies to her? Or is it about her winning? Or having power and control? Her attraction to Graham seems like it's always been more about his money and status than actual love. But if she has Graham, has a family, then she has it all. At least, it appears that way to everyone on the outside. And appearances are everything to her, aren't they?

It makes me sick.

Speaking of which...

"Now Jude, you can't possibly wear your riding boots to dinner. What will people think?" Natasha is saying. "Why don't you and the nanny hurry back to your closet to find something more appropriate?"

"But Mommy—"

"*Go change now,*" Natasha snaps, her voice so loud that even I jump.

"Come on," I say as gently as I can, leading Jude away by the hand.

We settle on a pair of black mary-janes, though Jude makes a face.

"I'd rather wear riding boots, too. But let's keep your mom happy," I tell her.

On the way there, Jude asks, "Are we going somewhere fun for dinner, Mommy?"

Natasha lifts a perfectly arched eyebrow and glances at me. "Don't you worry about a thing, darling. You'll have plenty of fun with your nanny along to entertain you."

I bite my tongue and offer a tight smile.

"Can I get scallops?" Jude prods, oblivious to the shade being thrown at me by her mom.

Graham ignores us all, typing what I assume is a work email on his iPad. My insides knot a little. It feels like the heart-to-heart we had earlier went in one ear and right out the other.

Natasha cups Jude's chin. "Of course. Whatever your little heart desires, Mommy will provide."

"Always with a string attached," Graham mutters under his breath.

"What was that, love?" Natasha asks with a bite, still smiling at Jude.

"I said I hope our name hasn't been scratched. From the reservation list." Graham checks his watch, refusing to be cowed by her thinly veiled attitude. "We're late, after all."

"Don't be silly. I'm Natasha Ratliff. Nobody's going to turn that name away." Natasha flashes a shark-like smile and turns her attention back to her phone, scrolling through the most recent reviews for her Broadway show. She's obsessed with her critics, I've noticed.

The remainder of the car ride over to Soho is filled with Natasha shit-talking any naysaying reviewers and detailing the glorious VIP parties she attended while we were gone. None of us could get in a word edgewise if we wanted to, but Jude mostly keeps her nose in her horse book and Graham spends his time tapping at his tablet. Natasha barely notices.

Finally, the driver drops us off outside a pretentious-looking glass, black steel, and marble-fronted restaurant called Piatto. As we walk inside, we get several looks that range from shock and awe—*Oh my God, it's Natasha Ratliff!*—to annoyance as they eyeball poor Jude bringing up the rear with her horse-shaped pocketbook. To her credit, the kid takes no notice.

We're immediately seated despite our tardiness, so I pull out a notebook that I keep in my bag for occasions exactly like this—when Natasha insists on dragging Jude along with her someplace that does not cater to children. I start playing tic-tac-toe and hangman with Jude, trying to keep her busy so she can't possibly get too boisterous and be accused of upsetting the other patrons, and as usual it works like a charm. Meanwhile, Natasha orders drinks and appetizers for everyone without consulting us.

Jude and I end up with Pellegrino water while Natasha and Graham share a bottle of wine.

Everything is going fine until the waiter takes our orders.

"I'll have the seafood risotto please," Jude says primly, peering up over her menu.

"We do not have *children's* risotto," the waiter says, clearly put out by the fact that the table in his section has a child sitting at it. He turns to Natasha. "Mrs. Ratliff, we do not have a children's menu. Perhaps our young guest would prefer some buttered pasta."

Jude lifts her chin and haughtily informs him, "Maybe *you* would prefer buttered pasta, but *I* am in the mood for scallops."

This makes me smile, and even Graham looks like he's fighting off a look of amusement.

"Hush," Natasha says dismissively, waving Jude's comment away before telling the waiter, "Buttered pasta would be perfect."

"I want the risotto, Mommy," Jude says, frowning. "It has scallops in it. You said I—"

"*Stop it*," Natasha snaps under her breath. "Don't be bitchy."

Jude's expression of mild upset instantly turns to one of shock. Even the waiter takes a step back. I can't believe Natasha just spoke to her child this way. It is, apparently, Graham's last straw as well.

"Do *not*," he growls quietly, "speak to my daughter that way. Ever."

Natasha turns slowly to look at him, a smile stretching across her harshly painted lips. Immediately, dread runs through me, icy cold. She and Graham are about to have a very nasty, very public argument in the middle of this restaurant. In front of their daughter.

In front of everyone.

"She's *my* daughter," Natasha says, escalating the conflict in a much louder voice. People at nearby tables look over, making me nervous. "You are *lucky* I am allowing you access."

Graham's whole body goes tense. "I think it's the other way around, sweetheart, unless what you're trying to say is that she is, in fact, the stable boy's daughter."

I gape. *Stable boy's daughter?* What the hell does that even mean?

Natasha narrows her eyes and slaps her menu down on the table.

"Jude, um, let's go to the restroom." I stand up and sling my purse over my shoulder, holding a hand out to Jude, desperate to hustle her out of the line of fire as quickly as possible.

"But I don't need to—okay, okay." Jude stumbles as I haul her up and drag her away with me, looking over her shoulder at her parents, who are already biting each other's heads off.

As we stand in front of the fancy baroque mirror in the ladies' room, Jude says, "Why are we in here? I hear them fight all the time."

"Maybe so, but it's no fun having to watch it, is it? Besides, I figured we could have ourselves a little primp session," I tell her as I work my pocket comb through her ponytail.

But through the door, we can still hear Graham and

Natasha shouting. I'm sure the entire restaurant—scratch that, the entire borough—can hear it too. I turn the water on, hoping to drown out some of the sound, but it doesn't do much.

"I want you and all your things out of my house! For good!" Graham is saying.

"You can't just kick me out!" Natasha yells, followed by the sound of breaking glass.

"You're lucky I don't kill you instead!" Graham shoots back. "Because it'd be a hell of a lot easier!"

I can't help wincing. In the mirror, I see Jude look down, her shoulders slumping.

"I really hate this," she whispers.

"I'm sorry," I tell her, spinning her around for a tight hug. "I'm sure it'll be over soon."

"What a sucky bummer," she mumbles into my chest.

I kiss the top of her head. "You said it."

Inside I feel nothing but tangled guts. I don't like their fights, either. My own parents had more than enough of them when I was growing up, though nothing quite like the Ratliffs'.

A few minutes later, it's quiet again. We decide to go back out to the table and see if the dust has settled, but despite her bravado, Jude still looks small and terrified. Just as I'm putting my purse back over my shoulder, I feel my phone vibrating from the inner pocket.

"Hold on a sec," I tell Jude, digging around for my cell.

I have a text from Graham. It reads, *Natasha stormed out and I'm getting in a cab. Enjoy dinner with Jude. My*

AmEx is with the waiter, and Ronaldo is standing by to come pick you up when you're done. PS- Get Jude dessert.

I frown at the text message. Dessert won't fix this. Not by a long shot.

"What's wrong?" Jude asks.

Putting on the brightest smile I can muster, I take her hand. "Nothing. Your parents had to go take care of some urgent business. It's just us two now. You ready for those scallops?"

She searches my eyes, then nods slowly, tightening her grip on my hand. We walk out together to find an empty table, a busboy sweeping glass off the floor nearby, and an entire room full of patrons trying to pretend they aren't watching us out of the corners of their eyes.

"Actually...tell you what," I say quietly. "Let's go get ice cream somewhere else."

"Ice cream for dinner?" Jude's eyes grow wide. "Really?"

"Really. We just need to find the waiter first so we can grab your dad's card."

As we slide into a bright purple booth with our sundaes minutes later at Van Leeuwen, it hits me hard: Graham kicked Natasha out. For good. Which means he hates her just as much as I do. No more kissing her ass and putting up with her abuse and her harsh treatment of Jude. It also means that from now on, it'll just be me and him and Jude at home.

Our home.

Finally.

Chapter Twenty-Two

Abbie

ICE CREAM for dinner may not have been the wisest choice.

Jude drifted off surprisingly easy as I read *Black Beauty* to her a few hours ago, but now I'm laying here in bed staring at the ceiling, wide awake from sugar and stress and worry. The apartment was empty when Jude and I got home, and Graham hasn't answered any of my calls or texts. I can only take comfort in the thought that he wouldn't just leave Jude here with Natasha after a fight like that, so I'm assuming he'll be back at some point. Still, my heart is racing.

Somehow, I manage to fall asleep, because the next thing I know, I'm waking to the familiar weight of Graham's body over mine, his woodsy scent, the feel of his lips on my neck.

"Mm," I moan softly, wrapping my legs around his waist. This is like a dream.

"Abbie," he murmurs.

His mouth covers mine, his kiss aggressive and almost

angry. I struggle to keep up. His hands slip up the back of my shirt, clawing at my skin. When he helps me sit up so he can pull the camisole over my head, I hear the fabric rip. Graham curses under his breath.

"Hey. Are you okay?" I murmur against his lips.

"I don't want to talk." He lays me back down on the bed a little less gently than I'd like and loosens his tie. "I need you."

"I need you too," I tell him, watching him all but tear his clothes off. The lights from outside cast shadows across his chiseled chest and abs, and when he takes off his glasses to toss them on the nightstand, I tease, "Where'd you go, Clark Kent?"

"He's gone. It's Superman now." He grabs my ankles to drag me closer to the edge of the bed, then slides off my panties and spreads my legs wide. "Don't wake Jude."

I smile. "I'll do my best."

Graham doesn't return my humor like I'd hoped, just drops to his knees. He immediately dives into my center, licking me hungrily like I'm an ice cream cone. Stifling a moan, I arch my back to nudge my nub against his teeth. He sucks hard on it and slips a finger inside me.

"Is Natasha coming back tonight?" I ask, fighting against the hesitation cropping up in my head despite the euphoria happening between my legs.

"I said I don't want to talk."

Damn his fucking stonewalled male stoicism. "Should we lock the door?"

He bites down hard enough on my clit to steal my breath. His brows are furrowed when he looks up at me. "No."

"Oh. *Oh.*" I moan as he slips another finger inside me and curls them toward my sweet spot.

I long for the day I don't have to worry about anyone walking in on us, and it's hard to stay focused on what he's doing because I'm so anxious we're going to be found out. Natasha was already unhinged at dinner. Who's to say she won't come barging in, looking to rip Graham a new asshole—only to have her suspicions confirmed?

"You're thinking too much." He runs the flat of his tongue against the length of my slit. "There's only room for one of us to do that."

"Sorry." I shake my head and try to let my fears go. "I can't help it."

"I'm not a good enough distraction?"

"I didn't say that."

"Good. Now hush," Graham commands.

I obey and lean back, mentally casting out everything on my mind except the view of Graham's head between my thighs. I feel one of his fingers slip down to my most sensitive hole and my entire body shivers at the contact.

"You like that?" he asks, slowly rubbing in circles. "Does my naughty girl like it when I toy with her asshole?"

"I thought you said no more talking," I toss out instead of answering.

This is brand new to me. He's only briefly touched me like this before...and with all of me spread wide before him, open and vulnerable, the sensations are overwhelming. When he slips his finger inside that tight ring, just a little, I have to force myself to relax. Then he starts pumping, gently. My God. I can't even tell if I like it, being invaded like this, but it's sure as hell doing a good job of distracting me.

His fingers increase their pace, filling all of my holes so perfectly I can't help panting. I throw my head back and thread my fingers through Graham's hair, grinding my clit against his tongue as I ride the thrusts of his fingers. I love this part. The delicious buildup. The part where hot little shocks of lightning start to strike at my center, where I know my orgasm is imminent, where I begin to lose myself in the fast-approaching storm.

"*Graham,*" I whisper, letting my body take over. "Yes, yes, yes."

He growls in response and the vibrations against my clit are almost enough to push me over the edge. My breath gets even faster and I close my eyes, picturing the night we made love at the estate under a sky like a blanket of stars, the warm summer air caressing our bare skin, and soon my mind goes blissfully dark. All I can see, taste, and feel is Graham.

"I'm coming," I warn him.

"Mmm," he murmurs.

One more well-placed nibble on my clit and the orgasm is washing over me in warm, tingling waves, my toes curling as my core tightens and relaxes over and over in rapid succession. I pull a pillow over my face to muffle my groans as he licks me through it, causing my entire body to convulse against him. It takes a few minutes for me to come down from the power of it all, to slow my panting and moaning to an acceptable level.

When I toss the pillow aside, I hear him laugh. It's quiet, but it's there.

"What's so funny?" I ask.

I sit up on my elbows, looking up at the beautiful sight of Graham standing naked over the foot of the bed.

"You," he whispers.

"Me?"

He crawls up the bed until his lips find mine, and this time his kiss is softer and slower and more passionate, gentle even. I fall into it, no longer worried about anything or anyone. I don't care who walks in on us, as long as he keeps kissing me just like this.

"You and that silly pillow," he whispers.

"I was told to be quiet and I obeyed," I point out.

"You were perfect."

Smiling, I wrap my legs around his hips, pulling him into me until I can feel his cock against my opening. I moan against his mouth, hungry for more. I'm so wet that Graham slides right into me. It feels like nothing short of magic. He presses his forehead to mine and we rock to an easy rhythm, his previous fire more of a smolder than a burn. Every time he thrusts into me, our eyes locked, I feel more and more connected to him.

"She's gone," he murmurs.

"What?" I don't immediately follow.

"Natasha." He kisses me again, hungrier than the last. "Everything is over. We're done."

Adrenaline pumps through me, but I'm too afraid to get my hopes up only to have them dashed, so I stay quiet and wait for him to say more. Buried inside me, he stops his thrusts and tilts my chin so we're eye to eye.

"I told her she's not coming back to the estate, Abbie. We go home tomorrow."

"Home," I whisper, a weight lifting off my chest.

It's exactly what I've dreamed of, isn't it? But it doesn't feel real. It's too good to be true.

I take a breath and then cup his face in my hands. "What does this mean, Graham? For us? Does this mean we can...actually be together?"

Even though I'm afraid of his answer, I can't keep living in this fantasy version of reality, telling myself I just need to be patient and that Graham and I will figure it all out later. I need his assurances. But more than that, I need the truth. Even if it hurts.

"There's no one else I want." His gaze is so intense it's like I'm staring into the sun. He thrusts inside me again and stays there, lowering his head to kiss me again. "If you'll have me?"

"I'll have you. Always."

We kiss softly, relentlessly, and fall back into our lovemaking. No more talking, no more words. It's soothing, reaffirming, the kind of sex that sounds simply vanilla, but in reality only seems to strengthen our bond.

We stay together all night, each climax like a fulfilled promise after all the time we've had to deny ourselves of this connection. Hours pass with us changing positions, massaging each other's bodies, biting and sucking and stroking each other, until we're finally too tired to move. I lose count of how many times I come.

Right as I'm about to drift off, snuggled against his side, I remember that there's something else he's kept from me—something else I need him to come clean about.

"Who ratted us out?" I ask, fighting sleep.

Graham wraps his arm tighter around me and kisses the top of my head.

"You're relentless."

"I am, yes. Just tell me so I can stop asking."

He sighs. "I've handled the situation already. He's been fired."

"He? So definitely not Esmeralda." Or Natasha, for that matter.

"One of the stable hands sold the story," Graham admits. "He's been having an affair with Natasha, apparently."

"What?" I gasp, suddenly wide awake. "Quinn?"

"Indeed."

Confusion and betrayal hit me hard. And...guilt. *I was the one who blabbed to Quinn about Graham and me on our so-called date, but only because I was trying to manifest it into reality.* Or, if I'm being honest, because I was being dumb and mouthy. I gave that asshole all the fodder he needed to blackmail the love of my life and destroy everything dear to him.

"That piece of shit," I hiss.

"Hush," Graham says firmly. "It's been handled."

He sounds grim. Now his comment at dinner about Jude not being his daughter suddenly makes sense.

I huff out a breath. "I hope that means you castrated him."

Graham chuckles and the sound sets me at ease. He tips my chin upward and kisses me gently. "My firecracker, that's enough worry for tonight. Now, you've worn out these old bones. Let's try to get some rest."

I snuggle close again and listen to him drop off to

sleep quickly, just like Jude does. His breathing evens out and a feeling of pure euphoria overtakes me as I drift away.

The last thing I think to myself is, this could be my life, every day. Forever.

So I'm going to do everything in my power to make that happen.

Chapter Twenty-Three

Abbie

I AWAKEN to find Graham tiptoeing around the room with a towel wrapped around his waist, his hair damp, gathering his clothes from last night off the floor. I catch the clean scents of my soap and coconut shampoo on the humid air leaking from the en-suite bathroom. The sky outside is lightening to a pre-dawn blue, but the sun's not quite up yet.

"Hey, you," I say softly.

He turns. "Sorry, I tried not to wake you. How'd you sleep?"

"Mmm. Like a baby."

"You earned it. Unfortunately, I have to go." He comes over to drop a kiss on my lips and then pulls his shirt over his head, which makes me a little sad.

"Stay with me."

Graham shakes his head and buttons his pants. "Can't. Jude will be up soon and the staff is already stirring. I'll see you at breakfast, and we'll talk logistics for heading home."

There's that word again. Home. It sends a warm rush through me.

I wrap a robe around myself and slide off the bed to see him out. But as soon as I open the door, I'm surprised to find Jude standing there in the hallway. My heart immediately starts pumping a million miles an hour. Graham freezes behind me.

"Mommy's not waking up," Jude says.

"Um. Thank you, Mr. Ratliff, for getting rid of that huge spider," I blurt, barely paying attention to what she said as I scramble for an excuse to be sneaking Graham out of my room at this hour. "Now I can go back to sleep."

Graham steps past me and nods. "Of course. Spiders don't scare me. Happy to help."

"Mommy won't wake up," Jude repeats, her voice reaching frantic octaves. "I think something's wrong."

Graham and I share a look, probably thinking the same thing. She's probably passed out from too much booze last night. Per usual. To say Natasha has an addictive personality is a gross understatement. Since living with her, I've realized she's almost never sober. Whatever vice she feels like partaking of that day (or night...or both), she embraces to the fullest.

"I'll go check on her," Graham says, the epitome of calm. "Where is she?"

"In bed." Jude's chin trembles.

"I'm sure she's fine, love," Graham soothes. He looks at me. "Abbie?"

"Come on, Jude. Let's go to the kitchen. Maybe we can see about making some pancakes."

"Okay..." Jude doesn't look convinced, but follows me obediently down the hall.

I can't tell her that her mother is an addict and probably sleeping off an entire bottle of Grey Goose mixed with whatever prescriptions she's on, so I try to do my best to distract her. I put music on the smart speaker and start rummaging through the pantry.

"I think something's really wrong," Jude says from the table, where she's hunched in a chair with a haunted look on her face.

"Oh, honey." I give her the biggest sympathetic look I can muster. "Sometimes grown-ups just need a lot of sleep. Your mom has been working really long hours with the show."

She doesn't say anything, just nods and picks at her fingernails.

"*Abbie.*" I turn to find Graham standing in the doorway, his face tight.

Jude stands up, face scrunched up in worry. An uneasy feeling floods through me.

"What's wrong with Mommy?" Jude asks.

"I just need Abbie for a moment," Graham tells her, but it's obvious by his expression that something is very, very wrong.

"I'll be right back, okay?" I give Jude's shoulder a squeeze.

"I'm coming, too," she protests loudly, heading toward the doorway.

"No," Graham says sharply, holding out his hand to stop her. "You're to stay here."

Jude freezes and then retreats to the chair again, sullen and nervous.

I follow Graham across the apartment, my adrenaline pounding. "What's going on?"

He doesn't answer, just pulls out his phone when we get outside Natasha's bedroom door. "Fucking hell. They are going to eat this up."

"What? Who will eat *what* up?"

"Natasha's out cold. I can't get her up. She's unresponsive," he says quietly, looking over his shoulder.

My heartrate doubles. "Is she...breathing okay?"

"Barely." He finishes dialing and puts the phone to his ear. "Hello, I need an ambulance. The address is..."

"An *ambulance*?" I whisper, but Graham puts his finger to his mouth as he finishes giving the person on the other end of the line the apartment address.

"She's unconscious, shallow breathing, her skin is cool to the touch. Yes, I'll hold."

"Oh my God, Graham—"

He puts a hand on my shoulder. "I need you to make sure Jude is okay. She's going to be very upset when the paramedics get here. I'll go in the ambulance; you and Jude can follow."

"Okay. I'll get her ready." I nod and head back down the hall. I can hear Graham speaking quietly to the 911 operator again as I go.

In the kitchen, Jude is sitting in front of a glass of water, looking even more stricken than before. As soon as she hears my footsteps, she jumps right up.

"I want to see my mom."

I freeze in place, unsure how to handle this. I won't lie to her, but I also don't know what to say that won't completely freak her out. I look at the poor girl, still in her pajamas.

"You're going to see her soon, but first let's go get you dressed," I say.

"What's wrong with her? Why won't anyone tell me what's going on?" Jude's voice is pitched high with panic.

Walking over to her, I look her right in the eye so she knows I'm not trying to hide anything. "She isn't feeling well, sweetie. She's going to see a doctor. Your dad called for help already and they're sending an ambulance over to pick her up."

Jude blinks back tears. "I want to see her!"

"Clothes first, okay? She's still asleep, so all we can do right now is go to the hospital and wait until they find out what's going on. Your dad will ride in the ambulance and you and I are going to take a car over right away."

She doesn't need to be told twice. Jude runs back to her room and starts pulling on her clothes from last night. I don't say anything about it, because I'm sure I'd be just as anxious to get out the door if I were her.

"Brush your teeth and maybe grab a book, too. We might be waiting for a while," I tell Jude. "I'm going to get ready in my room—stay here and I'll come back when I'm done."

I step out into the hallway and find Graham there. Before either of us can speak, there's a heavy, rapid knock at the front door. In a matter of minutes, the apartment is flooded with paramedics with bags, equipment, and a stretcher. Graham takes over, and I rush to get ready.

While I'm pulling on jeans and scrambling for

deodorant and mouthwash, I hear the EMTs asking Graham questions, their walkie-talkies blaring with static, and then the sound of a stretcher being rolled down the hall. Red and blue lights flash from the street outside, and my adrenaline is pumping so hard I feel dizzy.

My door swings open. Jude's standing next to Graham with tears running down her face.

"I've got to go. There's a car waiting downstairs for you two," Graham says. "It's Mount Sinai. Just go straight to the ER and I'll find you."

All I can do is nod as Graham leaves the apartment with the EMTs. Jude and I can hear the ambulance sirens pierce the air as we take an elevator down to the lobby. Her hand grips mine tightly, but on the whole ride over to the hospital, she doesn't say a word.

The ER waiting room is wall to wall beige, with rows of uncomfortable gray chairs. Graham is already there when we arrive, and he pulls Jude into a hug right away but tells her he doesn't know anything yet. I volunteer to find coffee and return to find Jude pretending to read her copy of *Black Beauty*, but it's obvious she can't focus since she barely turns the pages. Graham and I exchange grimaces over the hot black tar I bought in the cafeteria, but it's better than nothing.

As the minutes tick by, Jude gets increasingly antsy, so I attempt to distract her with a trip to the vending machines to get us some semblance of breakfast—though none of us are really in the mood to eat the bags of cheese crackers and granola bars and trail mix. We're all tense, and Jude alternates between crying and staring blankly at her book or the news on TV.

Finally, a doctor appears, looking for Graham.

"Abbie," he says quietly, rising from his chair, "take Jude to the restroom."

I nod and take her hand, and when we get back, Graham is pacing by a window. He frowns when he sees us, and I instantly know the news can't be good. Jude and I go over to him, and he wraps her in a hug.

"Did they find out what's wrong, Daddy?" Jude asks.

"They did," he tells her, his voice strained.

"What did the doctor say?" I ask.

"It's an overdose." He pulls back from Jude to look her in the eye. "Mommy's had too much medicine, love. That's why she's sick."

Jude's chin wobbles. "Did she wake up yet?"

"Not yet." His voice is grim. "She's still asleep. She's in a coma."

Chapter Twenty-Four

Graham

Marriage is a hell of a thing. You decide to build a life with someone, have kids, make a home. You and your partner share a bed, meals, your most intimate thoughts, secrets, dreams. You go on holidays together and pick out private schools. You're family. And then one day, the person you thought you'd spend forever with, the person who was going to hold your hand through life, has an affair and blows a hole right through the entire thing. Your partner becomes your enemy. Your home becomes a battlefield, the child a weapon. Forget holidays.

Divorce can be a gift, I think. For some.

All the same, I'll always love my ex-wife in some kind of way—we had a good run when we were younger, and she is Jude's mother, after all. But right now, Jude is a mess, and I'm fucking furious at my ex-wife for putting us all in this position.

I should have realized Natasha had a drug problem. I should have intervened, pushed her to get help. Yes, I knew she drank too much; Natasha frequently relied on alcohol to get through the day, even though the world was her proverbial oyster. But drugs? I never imagined.

At my request, and with a generous opening of my wallet, we've been moved to a private waiting room. Abbie sits in the corner, reading some horse book to Jude. My daughter has barely said a word since the doctor came to deliver the bad news. As for me, I can't stop vacillating between shock and anger and a kind of desperate panic that I'm not at all used to.

Even unconscious, Natasha continues to destroy our lives. How dare she do this. How dare she cause this harm to our child. How dare she make such a fucking fuss because *she* was, and is, unfaithful. Because *she* took the steps to dissolve our life together. Because *she* got so stuffed to the gills with opioids that she's now hooked up to countless machines that beep and hiss, terrifying Jude to no end.

I need to go for a run. Empty my mind, exhaust myself, focus on nothing but burning muscles and lungs and the cycle of my breath. Yet all I can do is pace the length of this room for the hundredth time, trapped in this purgatory. Praying for this relentless waiting to end.

"Is she going to die?" I hear Jude stutter across the room, sniffling and wiping her nose with a tissue Abbie hands to her.

"Nobody knows the answer to that, not even the doctors," I say, harsher than I intended. Abbie shoots me a look, so I try for a more soothing tone. "All we can do is wait right now."

Jude nods as Abbie pulls her onto her lap and smooths her hair back. "Everyone's taking really good care of your mom, okay? So try not to worry. I know it's hard."

"I'm scared," Jude is whispering into Abbie's neck.

Abbie rubs circles on Jude's back and tells her, "It's okay to be scared. This is scary. But you know what? You saved your mom's life today. She's here with all these great doctors and nurses taking care of her because of you."

She shoots me another look and tilts her head toward Jude, as though she's expecting me to come over and say something as well. God, Abbie is so much better at this whole comforting thing than I am. What is there for me to say, even? My concern for my daughter is still vastly outweighed by my fury at Natasha.

And I know I certainly can't give voice—even in my darkest thoughts—to how much better it would have been if Natasha had just died. This would have been a clean break. A fresh start for us all. We could already be in the process of healing our wounds and moving forward.

I shake away my guilty musing and take a seat next to Jude, resting my hand on her knee. "Abbie's right. You've been very brave, Jude."

"Thank you." Her voice is small.

"No, thank *you* for looking out for your mother." Even though we'd all be a lot fucking better off without her. "I'm so proud of you."

Jude rests her small hand on mine and squeezes tight. Each squeeze of her hand propels the dagger of anger further into my heart. Natasha did this to Jude. She did this to me. She doesn't deserve saving.

A firm knock at the door interrupts my thoughts, and

all of us whip around expecting to see a doctor or a nurse, come to deliver the latest on Natasha. Instead, it's two navy-uniformed police officers who step into the room.

"Mr. Ratliff?" the female officer says, her commanding voice making Jude visibly shrink back on Abbie's lap. "May we have a word?"

I nod. "Of course."

The officer glances at Jude and Abbie before adding, "Privately."

My stomach starts to churn. The last thing I need is for Jude to be even more upset by witnessing whatever is about to happen. Pulling out my wallet, I remove a few bills and hand them to Abbie.

"Can you take Jude out of here for a few minutes, please?" I ask quietly. "Maybe a visit to the cafeteria? It's getting to be lunchtime anyway. She can have whatever she wants."

"Daddy? What's going on?" Jude says anxiously.

Abbie takes Jude's hand, her eyes darting back and forth between the police. "Nothing to worry about, Jude. We're going to grab a quick snack while your dad talks to these officers. Maybe we can even find some cake."

"Do you think they have carrot cake?" Jude asks softly.

"They might. Only one way to find out." Jude looks to me, back at Abbie, and then nods. Abbie takes her hand. "We'll be back soon."

She keeps her voice light, surely for Jude's benefit, but I can tell by the set of Abbie's fine jaw that she's tense. Scared, even.

As soon as they're gone and I'm alone with the cops, I

gesture at the empty chairs and lower myself into one. "So. How can I help you?"

The woman steps forward, and I assume judging by her graying hair and sharp eyes that she has seniority over the clean-shaven, baby-faced guy she's partnered with. "We'd like you to come back to the precinct with us and answer some questions. Give an official statement on Mrs. Ratliff."

Bollocks. A statement? I straighten my cufflinks. "Is this something we can do here?"

"Afraid not," the younger cop says, not unkindly.

I frown. We still don't know much about Natasha's condition, but at the same time, all the sitting and fretting and imagining the worst is really wearing on Jude, and it's obvious there's nothing we can do here at the hospital. Perhaps it's time we all had a proper break.

"All right. Let me make sure my daughter gets home safely and then I'll be happy to come in and answer—"

The older officer holds up her hand to stop me. "Our patrol car is just outside, Mr. Ratliff. We'll wait for you."

They'll *wait for me*? So they don't even trust me to get myself to the police station on my own? What the hell is this? I take a breath and force myself to remain calm. Showing any signs of aggression or outrage toward these cops will only make me look worse.

"Very well. If you'll just give me a moment to make a call," I say, already dialing Abbie.

She picks up immediately.

"Abbie. I need to go with the police and answer some questions about Natasha. Can you get Jude back to the estate? I'll have Ronaldo come with the car."

"Okay, yeah...if you think that's best. Maybe the change of scenery will be good for her." She lowers her voice. "Are you going to be okay?"

"I'm fine," I assure her. "It's just formalities."

She and Jude return minutes later, plastic containers of cake in their hands, and I give the briefest explanation I can. When I tell Jude she'll have to leave without me, she balks, but I'm able to convince her to go by promising that I'll be right behind her and Abbie.

"And we'll come back to the hospital as soon as we hear something solid from your mother's medical team," I add.

I hold her hand tightly as we make our way through the main lobby, flanked by police officers, and find a wall of paparazzi waiting for us outside. The bastards are circling like buzzards over a carcass.

"Get her to the car as fast as you can," I tell Abbie. "Don't let them stop you. Jude, put your hood up."

"I don't want to go without you!" Jude grabs my arm.

"I'm sorry, but I have to meet with some people first." I scoop her into a hug, well aware that the cops all around us are watching my every move. "Go with Abbie like we agreed. You can eat your cake in the car. I'll be there as soon as I can."

"But Daddy—"

"Come on, Jude," Abbie coaxes. "Cassie is going to have Desi ready for you as soon as we get there. We'll spend the afternoon with the horses while we wait for your dad."

"Okay." Jude frowns as she surveys the writhing mass of cameras and reporters outside.

I give her one last squeeze and set her down, preparing to face the onslaught. I nod to the police officers with whom I'll be riding to the station, then step out the doors with the older woman in front of me and the younger, greener one trailing behind, hoping I can distract the media from the girls heading to their waiting car with their own police escort.

"Graham! Mr. Ratliff! Mr. Ratliff!" they all shout as the world explodes with flashbulbs.

"What happened to Natasha?"

"Where was she last night?"

"Graham!" a paparazzo shouts, stepping directly in front of me. "Everyone heard you threaten your wife at Piatto last night. Did you try to kill her?"

My eyes find Jude up ahead, ducking into the back seat of the black town car with Abbie. Turning back to the paparazzo, my blood boiling, I can't help but sneer.

"Have a little class. The only way I planned to hurt my wife was by enforcing our prenup—she cheats, she gets nothing."

The officers and I have reached their patrol car, and the younger guy is kind enough to simply open the back door for me rather than try to push me inside or otherwise make a scene. Even so, I shudder to imagine all the headlines tomorrow, accompanied by these photos of me being taken away by the cops.

"Do you expect to be formally charged, Mr. Ratliff?" a reporter shouts, just as I'm about to slide into the back of the patrol car.

Looking over my shoulder, I shout back, "What I

expect is that you'll have a little respect for our daughter. Now back off."

As we sit in New York City traffic the whole way to the station, all I can think is, when did this become my life? And how the hell did it get so bad? But I already know the answer.

Because I let Natasha destroy it. I let her walk back into my house and threaten me, succumbing to all her demands in the false hope that I could make peace with her long enough to figure out how to keep custody of Jude. Except it did no good—reconciling with Natasha, even if it was just for show, only made things worse. So much worse.

I should have never taken her back in. I should have taken the rumors on the chin and told the world they were created by a scorned Natasha. She's already fodder for the tabloids, they would have taken it and run.

Instead, I may have made the worst mistake of my life.

Chapter Twenty-Five

Abbie

ESMERALDA AND CASSIE are waiting for us when we arrive at the estate. They both look worried, but to their credit they break into smiles and offer hugs when we get out of the car. Jude's mood seemed to elevate the tiniest amount as soon as the house came into view, but she's still pretty tense and subdued.

"How are you doing, Jude?" Esmeralda asks.

"I'm okay," she says with a shrug.

"Do you want to go see your horses, or hang out here at the house?" Cassie asks.

Neither of them mention Natasha, and I'm so grateful. I don't want Jude to dwell on it any more than she already is, because there's simply nothing to be done. I have no idea what will happen when Graham arrives, either, but I don't want Jude to spend the whole day panicking. She's had more than enough of that since this morning.

Jude's brows furrow. "I want to see Desi. I don't know if I feel like riding, though."

"That's okay," I tell her. "Whatever you want to do."

I can see the wheels turning in her head, and then she says, "Maybe I'll go change into my riding clothes, though. Just in case."

She heads inside, leaving me with Cassie and Esmeralda and Ronaldo, who's now leaning against the side of the car with his mouth pressed into a hard line.

Cassie looks over her shoulder to be sure Jude is out of earshot and then asks what I'm sure they're all wondering. "How bad was it? Natasha's...accident...has been all over the news. I'm sure Jude's been freaking out."

I sigh. "Obviously this is all confidential, but it can't be worse than what the press is probably going to say, so... Jude found her mom unconscious this morning. Graham called an ambulance and we've basically just been sitting around at the hospital all day. The only thing the doctors could tell us is that she OD'd."

"On what?" Cassie whispers.

"I don't know. Graham's the one who's been talking with the doctors. Some kind of prescription painkillers. I don't know if they were hers or something recreational. Which, mixed with the amount of alcohol she drinks...I guess I'm just surprised this hasn't happened before."

Esmeralda shakes her head. "Enough of this talk. It won't do any good to speculate. What matters most is Jude, and getting her through this, however it goes. Thank God for you, Abbie."

My cheeks go hot. "She's a sweetheart. I'm lucky to have her, not the other way around."

"Nonsense." Esmeralda nudges me. "She's gone through plenty of nannies over the years, and none of them have connected to her like you do. Remember what she was like at the beginning of the summer? That poor child. You've helped her remember how to have fun."

"That means a lot," I say, my eyes dropping to the ground. "Really."

They have no idea why I originally took on this position, or what my ulterior motives were, but I still feel like shit about it. I don't deserve the praise.

Ronaldo tells us he'll be around if we need anything at all, and after everyone swears not to repeat anything I said about Natasha, he gets back in the car to take it to the garage.

"If Jude's feeling up to it, I was thinking I'd take her on a short ride before dinner," Cassie says, rescuing me from my conflicted feelings. "Wanna come?"

"Maybe. I'm fine just doing whatever Jude wants. I might take her swimming later, too. Anything to distract her. You're both welcome to join," I tell her and Esmeralda.

That gets a smile out of Esmeralda. "We'll see. For now, I need to find Mary and tell her she can get started on dinner. She's making sticky rice dumplings—one of Jude's favorites."

We part ways, Cassie to the stables to ready the horses, Esmeralda to the kitchen, and me to my room to change. After I pull my hair in a ponytail, I make my way to Jude's room. The door is shut, so I knock gently.

"Jude?"

"One second!" she calls. A moment later, she throws open the door. "All ready."

"You look great," I tell her, pretending not to notice

the pile of used, crumpled tissues on her bed, or how red her eyes are. "Let's go."

The whole way to the stable, she talks about horses. I do my best to chime in and draw her out, anything to keep her spirits up. Both of us are pleased to find that Cassie hasn't taken down the Christmas decorations, and soon enough Jude is in Desi's stall, chatting up her favorite horse. In minutes, Jude and I are following Cassie across the property. Our horses seem to revel in the lazy afternoon light spilling over the mountains as they canter over the green fields.

When we reach the trailhead, Cassie lets Jude take the lead. She urges Desi forward with a little whoop of delight and Cassie and I follow, exchanging looks of amusement. As we all make our way along the creek, under the shady canopy of old growth, trees, and through the expansive pastures, I think to myself once again how gorgeous the property is. I've never felt more fortunate than right now to be here. But how long can it last?

I used to fantasize about being with Graham forever, moving here permanently, becoming a part of the family for real. Now? I can't help worrying that what happened with Natasha means all my dreams are off the table. What if Graham feels guilty about her brush with death and decides to stay with her for Jude? What if he realizes he still loves her? What if I'm simply too much of a liability to have around, now that the media has its hooks in the ongoing saga of the Ratliff family? I don't know if I'll ever be seen as anything but the nanny, the homewrecker, an opportunistic gold digger. My relationship with Graham might be over and done with before it's even truly begun.

And then I silently chastise myself for even having these thoughts at all. The only person I should be thinking of is Jude, not myself. She's the one who's suffering the most. She's the one whose future happiness is riding on Natasha's recovery the most. I should be ashamed of myself.

Cassie must notice my brooding. She tries to distract me with stories about her most recent failed Tinder dates, but the sinking in my gut won't go away and my laughs are all forced.

Jude and I have a nice enough dinner, with the promised dumplings served alongside red bean soup and sauteed shrimp and crispy green beans with garlic, but Jude doesn't have much of an appetite. As for me, I can't stop peeking at my phone under the table to see if Graham has texted—which of course he hasn't. Neither Jude nor I have heard from him in hours, and my mind is racing with images of him getting interrogated, hand-cuffed, and thrown in a jail cell.

It's not until later, while Jude and I are sitting at the edge of the pool dipping our feet in, that she finally asks what I'm sure she's been worried about since we left the city.

"Why isn't my dad home yet? And why did the police take him away?"

"They didn't take him away," I tell her as calmly as I can, hugging her to me. "He just needed to answer some questions. I'm sure it's been a super busy day. He'll be home soon."

"But what if they put him in jail?" Jude's lower lip quivers a little.

"They won't," I say, even though her worries are identical to mine. "Why don't we try calling him again, okay? And if he doesn't pick up, we can leave another message."

But Graham doesn't pick up, and he doesn't make it home until hours after I put Jude to bed, clutching her stuffed horses and staining her pillow with tears. I read her as much *Black Beauty* as I could and stroked her hair until she finally drifted off, way past her usual bedtime. I can't believe the Natasha debacle was just this morning... this has been the longest day ever.

It's almost midnight when a familiar knock finally comes at my bedroom door. I race to open it and find Graham standing there, disheveled and exhausted and looking more stressed out than I've ever seen him. Before he even speaks, I jump into his arms and bury my face in his neck. I hold back my tears, clinging to him, breathing him in.

"God. I was so worried they wouldn't let you come home," I murmur.

"They couldn't keep me there," he says, walking me into the room and kicking the door closed behind us. But he doesn't let go of me. "But they certainly wanted to."

I pull back, searching his eyes. "Why? You were with *me*. We spent the whole night together, how can you be a suspect?"

"I'm not involving you in this," Graham says firmly. "Not after what the tabloids did to you last time. I said we were all asleep, which is the truth, and that's all there is to it."

"Okay. Well, they believed you, right? I mean, they let you go..."

Graham says nothing, but tugs at my shirt. I let him pull it over my head and unclasp my bra as I kiss him hard.

"It's going to be okay," I whisper, leading him to the bed.

"I just want to forget today happened."

"In that case, I might know a few ways to distract you."

I push him onto the mattress and then slowly undress him, taking my time to run my hands all over his body, kneading his tense muscles and dropping kisses over every plane and angle. Once he's completely naked, I make him lie back so I can crawl over him and take his rigid cock in my mouth. It's still one of my favorite ways to get to him, still gives me that boost of power that I crave as I make him writhe and gasp under the force of my tongue. I tease him less than I usually do, sucking and bobbing aggressively hard, knowing he needs this release more than ever before. I want to give him that oblivion, that sweet relief. But it takes him twice as long to come tonight, and his groans are harsher, almost as if he's in pain. By the time I've swallowed every last drop down, my lips are numb and my jaw aches.

Afterward, he sighs heavily. "I'm sorry. I...think I needed that."

"Don't apologize," I say climbing on top of him to a sitting position. "I'm not done with you yet. Not by half."

Graham looks up at me and cups my cheek, trailing his fingers over my swollen lower lip and then down my neck, between my breasts, all the way to my clit. I lean back with my palms on his thighs to steady myself, spreading my legs wide, giving him full access. When he pushes a finger inside me, I don't wait for him to find my sweet spot. Instead, I start rocking back and forth, fucking his finger with my wet pussy. Letting my head drop back, my eyes close.

"I don't want to be quiet," I tell him in between moans. "I want you to make me scream."

He reaches for me with his free hand and grabs my hair, pulling me down toward him for a kiss. "Naughty girl."

"You love it," I say, grabbing his cock.

He's hard again and ready for me, and I'm more than ready for him.

"I do," he says, hissing as I feed his length into me.

Graham flips me onto my back and starts thrusting, hard and fast, jackhammering into me with pure need. I come within minutes, needing him just as badly. Then we go again, gentle and slow, making love, and all the while he kisses me like there's no one else in the entire world.

And for those few hours, there really isn't.

Chapter Twenty-Six

Graham

NEW YORK CITY is buzzing this morning. Traffic is always terrible, of course, but it seems extra terrible today, like the City knows I don't want to be here. It fights me the whole way to the hospital, red lights and gridlock and wayward pedestrians every which way the driver turns. Everyone in the car is quiet, out of reverence or exhaustion, I don't know, but either way the silence weighs heavy.

Jude plays on her tablet as the City snaps us up in its foul jaws, and I spend the remainder of the trip watching Abbie from the corner of my eye. She's been so strong and unwavering, a calming presence in the chaotic mess that is my life. I don't know what I'd do right now without her. And Jude—she's never been so enamored with a nanny before. Neither, I suppose, have I.

How, I wonder, did this happen? She's so much younger than I am, bright-eyed and unmarred by life, without the chip on her shoulder that so many women my age seem to carry. It's not misogyny to say so; I know that chip well myself. I carry mine like a badge of honor, honed and sharpened from too many years of resenting my father, scrabbling to make it in the world, and then the bitterness of post-divorce living. But Abbie's freshness and pure innocence softens my edges. I feel vibrant again. I feel like *me* again.

That sort of thing can't be bought. No matter how many companies I acquire or how much money my banking empire amasses, I can't just go out and find that youthful vibrancy again. But with Abbie? The world is my oyster again. I can climb any mountain and sail any ocean with her by my side. She reinvigorates me. She makes me feel like I can start all over again, in the best way possible.

Dare I say I've felt like my old self, in ways I haven't felt in years. The sex is incredible. Her kisses bring me to my knees. Just the thought of her brings a smile to my face—as it does even now, during this interminable drive to Mount Sinai. And seeing her bring fun and joy into Jude's life again is one hell of an aphrodisiac all on its own. I don't know exactly when I fell for Abbie, I just know that it was pointless trying to fight it for as long as I did.

Suddenly, the sum of it all hits me full force, nearly taking my breath away. I love her.

I love her kindness, her patience, her way with my child. Her sense of humor, her sass, and her wicked sex drive. I love her laugh, her scent, her ripe cunt, her insatiable hunger for me.

I can't escape it. I'm in love with my daughter's nanny. I love Abbie Montgomery.

And things were all starting to finally fall into place...

Until fucking *Natasha*. Just as I was beginning to get back on my feet and find happiness and connection again, Natasha had to come along and pour gasoline all over my life—just so she could throw a match on it and watch the fire burn down everything I hold dear.

When I got the call this morning about her vitals, I'd held my breath, wondering if I was about to find out that she didn't make it through the night. I wasn't granted such kindness. And yes, I know I'm a bastard for thinking it.

Ronaldo drops us off outside the hospital and we hustle quickly inside, hoping to avoid any paparazzi who might be lurking nearby. As we make our way through the monotonous off-white halls, Jude clutches a sheet of notebook paper to her chest. Abbie offers to keep it safe in her purse for Jude, but she just holds it tighter and shakes her head. I suspect it's something for her mother, which stirs queer feelings. Of course Jude loves Natasha, she's her mother. But does Natasha love Jude as fiercely and unconditionally? That, in and of itself, is questionable.

There are all kinds of mothers, of course. All kinds of ways to parent and all kinds of love. However, Natasha never showed any maternal instinct. She hired a nanny two weeks after she gave birth, unable to keep up with the demands of a newborn, and had Jude on baby formula from day one. And I supported all her decisions, despite any lingering anxiety or misgivings, as this was our first child and both of us were still learning the ropes.

Much to my surprise, I found that feeding Jude

myself was a wondrous thing. That jumping up in the middle of the night when she woke us with her cries gave me a surge of adrenaline, the urge to soothe and protect her overtaking me instantly. New fatherhood seemed to fit me to a T, banishing all my fears that I'd loathe it like my own father anecdotally had.

Natasha, though. She seemed to grow less and less interested in Jude with each day that passed. She told me she felt trapped and overburdened, that she felt resentment toward the baby. Resentment toward me.

So instead of bonding with Jude, she decided what she needed most was to return to her old way of life as soon as possible. Go back out with her friends, galivant around Manhattan, increase her anxiety meds and resume her alcohol intake, and apparently (as I learned later) fuck anyone who looked at her twice. When she began the affair that would ultimately end our marriage, she left Jude and I without a second thought, packing a bag and never looking back. She barely came to visit unless there was a film or theatre premiere she needed to borrow Jude for, parading her around like a piece of jewelry with the power to give herself an extra glow.

Natasha is not, and never has been, a proper mother. She doesn't deserve Jude.

Now, I watch her carefully tape her sheet of paper to the head of Natasha's bed. It's a colorful drawing of Jude and Natasha, holding hands and surrounded by horses. Seeing it makes me smile. My daughter's devotion to her horses is one of the purest things about her.

"Dad?" Jude says, looking over her shoulder at me.

"Yes, love?" I shake my head slightly to clear out the cobwebs.

"Do you think Mommy can hear us?"

"That's what the doctor said."

Jude's face scrunches up for a moment, and then she positions herself beside Natasha, tentatively placing her hand over her mother's. She pushes up on her toes, kisses Natasha's cheek, and whispers, "I love you, Mommy. Please wake up soon."

It is a dagger to my soul and makes me hate my ex-wife all the more. So, I turn to look at Abbie. My lighthouse in the storm.

"Keep talking to her," Abbie encourages Jude gently. "Tell her to keep fighting."

Jude looks at me, her eyes watery. "Can I sit with her?"

I turn to the nurse in the room, who nods, and then help Jude climb carefully onto the bed. She snuggles beside her mother, careful to mind the IV and the various tubes and wires, and begins telling her about all the horses in the stables, about their mane ribbons and the Christmas decorations she and Cassie put up. She talks to Natasha like she's never even talked to me, like they are the dearest of friends, and it hurts my heart. I have never seen Jude have a conversation like this with her mother, and I wish it were a common occurrence, not an outlier.

"Want to get some air?" Abbie asks quietly at my elbow. "I think Jude could use some quiet time with her mom."

"She's stable," the nurse says. "If you need to step outside, Mr. Ratliff, please do."

I let out a breath. Abbie's right. Jude needs this time. "Will you be okay by yourself for a few minutes, Jude?"

"Yeah," Jude whispers, stroking her mother's hair.

"Very well. I'll be back soon. Abbie?"

She nods. "I wouldn't mind a walk."

I wish I could take her hand, let the reassuring warmth of her palm against mine render me grounded and unlost, but there are cameras and people everywhere. I cannot be seen fraternizing with my nanny in such a way after everything that's happened, and it enrages me even more that I cannot live my life by my own rules, all because of Natasha and her stable boy.

Instead, Abbie and I head down the hall side by side, keeping a respectable distance apart. I don't know what compels me, but I quietly say, "I wish I could take your hand."

The way her cheeks turn pink brings me a small flicker of joy. She brushes her pinkie against my palm, just briefly, and says, "I do, too."

"This situation is not ideal." I mean it as an apology. "You didn't sign up for any of this."

"It's my job. Well. It's more than that." She glances over at me, and I see the emotion in her eyes. Jude and I are her family; I feel the truth of it with every fiber of my being.

"I understand," I tell her.

We round a corner and start down another nearly identical hospital hallway, alive with beeps and fast walking nurses with quiet white shoes and stethoscopes hung around their necks. It puts me on edge, all the death and chaos that imbues this massive building.

There's something else on my mind, something else that's been bothering me. "I also...I know how Natasha treated you, Abbie, and your actions here in the hospital speak loudly about your character. I appreciate you. Jude and I, we...we're both grateful to have you."

"And I you," Abbie says softly.

"You're exquisite," I can't stop myself from blurting.

She blushes, and says nothing more.

We turn another corner and find a blissfully silent hallway. Next to us is an empty room, so I pull Abbie into it and shut the door behind us. In the dark, I press her back against the door and kiss her with the force of all the churning emotions in my gut. I kiss her to forget everything that's happened in the last two days. To tell her with my lips what I can't yet say with my voice.

"What was that for?" she whispers breathlessly, leaning her head against my chest.

"You deserve so much more than this hiding," I tell her. "Afraid of being seen, of getting caught. But this is all I can give you at the present."

"I'll take it," she says, reaching to pull my mouth back down to hers.

In that moment, I almost tell her I love her. Almost.

Chapter Twenty-Seven

Abbie

"ABBIE!" A familiar voice squeals just before I'm tackled by a huge hug.

"AMANDAAA!" I squeal back and let myself get lost in her arms, relieved and comforted and finally at home with my best friend.

We haven't seen each other all summer, and that is entirely too long. This was supposed to be the time of year that we spent all day at the pool, checking out guys and vegging out on tabloids, not the summer where I spent every waking moment working and *dodging* those tabloids. To have an entire day off to spend with my best friend is exactly what I need. I'm so grateful she made the two-hour drive from her parents' house in Stamford just to see me.

"Oh my God, are you crying?" Amanda squeezes me harder. "Stop it, or you'll make *me* cry."

"I'm not crying!" I sniff. "My eyes are leaking joy."

"Well my eyes are allergic to wet and this mascara isn't waterproof, so turn those taps off," she teases.

"I missed your stupid ass so much."

She grins. "I missed your stupider ass more."

I shake my head. "Impossible."

"Your mom is impossible," she shoots back.

"Don't tell hard truths when we're joking around!" It's my turn to tease her.

Amanda throws her head back and laughs, her mass of tight curls flying, and for the first time in months, my soul feels weightless.

Graham makes me feel impossible things all the time, but weightless is almost never one of them. We have to hide our relationship from literally everyone and that kind of stress is nothing if not heavy. But right now, with my best friend? I could walk on air.

"I can't believe this is it," she says, looking over my shoulder at the Ratliff estate. "It looks like the cover of a damn magazine."

"Do you want the tour?" I ask.

"Maybe later, but right now I'm frickin' starving. Get in the car, Cinderella."

I practically dive into the passenger seat and then play navigator, directing Amanda toward town. "So what are you in the mood for?"

"Lunch and then shopping? But first, lunch. A long lunch. A *ladies'* lunch."

"Sounds perfect," I say. "Maybe we should try to find a restaurant close to wherever you want to shop. There are tons of antique stores all over the place, the big outlet center on Route 32, that huge-ass fancy mall down in West Nyack..."

"What about lingerie shopping?" She lifts a brow at

me suggestively. "Since, you know, we could both use some right now."

"*Hold up, what*?" I look over with my eyes wide. "Are you saying you're actually seeing someone and you somehow failed to mention it to me until now?"

Amanda suddenly goes uncharacteristically quiet, her cheeks pinking by the second. "I don't know if I'd call it serious just yet, but I didn't want to jinx it. It's only been a few weeks."

"Girl, I am your very best friend. I don't jinx shit." I stick my lip out to pout. "You have to tell me everything."

"You should talk! I haven't gotten an update on Mr. Sexy British Lover in forever!" Then the smile drops off her face and she gives me a sympathetic look. "I mean, it's not like I haven't seen all the crap on the news recently. I just figured you'd give me the rundown when you were ready. Except with the whole OD thing going on...well. It didn't seem like the right time to harass you for hot gossip. I do have some self-control, you know."

I exhale deeply. "It's just as bad as it looks. With Natasha in a coma and everything, we can't exactly go public. And they got in this huge public fight at a restaurant the night before, which makes Graham look like shit. He had to leave the hospital to give a fucking statement to the police."

"God, I'm so sorry." Amanda reaches over and gives my hand a squeeze. "You don't have to talk about it if you don't want to."

"Thanks. I could use the break. With Jude, the *only* thing she wants to talk about is her mom, and when she's going to get better. The poor kid is a mess. Which, of course she is. I feel awful for her. There's just this sense of, like...suspension. Like we're all holding our breath.

"And Graham and I are basically right back to hiding everything again. I know he cares about me, but I can't plan for any kind of future with him when we're stuck in this holding pattern. But it's temporary, right? That's what I keep telling myself."

"It *is* temporary. Just don't forget that the fall semester starts next month. Not trying to be a downer, but I am not letting you drop out of an Ivy League college over this guy."

"I know. I'll figure it out," I say softly, a sick feeling twisting in my gut. "Anyway. Enough about me. Time to change the subject." I scowl at her playfully. "You owe me so many stories about this mysterious new lover of yours."

Amanda flushes bright red and says she'll tell me over lunch. I'm a little shocked—I've never known her to be shy about anything before. Especially not a guy. In our friendship, I'm the one who's always been weighed down by anxiety and social pressure, while Amanda shuns all of it to live loudly.

We end up parking near a fancy lingerie store with great Yelp reviews called Plume, and then walk to a nearby Italian place to get food first. Amanda orders us a million things to share, from a fried broccoli appetizer to white pizza and Moroccan salmon to dulce de leche cheesecake for dessert, which she makes me swear I'll save enough room for. We glug down our iced teas as we relax into the heavy air conditioning, a refreshing escape from the humidity outside.

"I know you're hungry, but there's no way we'll be able to eat all of that," I mock-scold her as the waiter walks away.

She rolls her eyes. "That's what to-go boxes are for. Besides, the point is to *taste* everything. Not finish it."

"I feel like that might actually be your entire life philosophy," I tease. "Now tell me about this mysterious gentleman. Do I know him?"

"Um. It's just...someone from my first-year writing seminar. Nobody you know. There's not much to tell yet, anyway." Amanda scratches the back of her neck, then looks away, then looks back at me and throws on another smile.

I have known this girl for half a decade, and I have never seen her like this. She's hiding something. Is it...one of my shitty exes? One of hers? Is he that much older, or —younger?

"He's over eighteen, right?" I ask nervously. "And under sixty-five?"

Amanda just laughs. "That's an appropriate age range. Oops, here comes our appetizer."

We spend the rest of our lunch date talking and laughing, and I don't bring up the new boyfriend again. I don't feel right pushing her about something she's so obviously uncomfortable sharing, even though it hurts to know she's keeping a secret from me. Hopefully, she'll let her guard down and come around soon. It'd be nice to have someone else's relationship to focus on.

Stuffed to the gills and swearing off cheesecake for the rest of our lives, we head back out into the heat and make our way to the lingerie store. The outside looks almost Parisian, with a gorgeous light stone façade and big windows and a classy sign with swirling script. Inside, we find row upon row of lace and silk underthings in every color of the rainbow. They also have gorgeous robes, pajamas, slippers, perfume, the scent of fresh flowers in vases enveloping us.

"This place is like literal heaven," I sigh to Amanda. "I don't even know where to start."

She gravitates toward a deep pink garter set near the front and runs her fingers across the satin rosettes at the hips. It has a lace-up corset top with little bows on the straps, which is a bit much for me, but for Amanda it's a match made in heaven.

"That one's a yes," I tell her. "It's so you. You'll look like one of those fancy little cakes from the *Marie Antoinette* movie."

She laughs and loops the hanger over her finger. "How about you? Something subtle, right? A shorty set. Cream, maybe powder blue?"

My cheeks go hot. "Oh, God. Am I that obvious?"

"Definitely. But I'm also your best friend."

That's when I look over and notice a guy standing on the other side of the plate glass window, dressed all in black with a red baseball cap, messing with a professional-looking camera. My pulse quickens and I retreat further into the store, hoping to disappear into the racks. Amanda follows, looking over her shoulder.

"Are you okay?"

"I'm fine." I try, and mostly fail, to shrug it off. "I just don't like cameras after...everything."

"Well, yeah. Your picture was plastered everywhere."

Amanda lowers her voice. "I mean, nobody wants to be famous like that. I'd be paranoid, too."

"I mostly feel bad for Jude." I cast a glance outside and the guy is gone. I take a deep breath and try to relax. He's probably just some tourist. Why would I think he was here to follow me? *Get a grip, Abbie.* "She's so young and they eat her up."

"Assholes," Amanda mutters. She picks up a black one-piece with dominatrix vibes and holds it up to her chest. "What do you think?"

"Hard to say without knowing the recipient." I wink at her. "But it's nice."

Amanda sighs and goes to look at herself in the mirror. "It is nice. I don't know. Maybe—" Her face goes slack and she turns around slowly. "He's back. The camera guy."

I very carefully shift my body, acting as though I'm looking at another rack, and sneak a look through the door. Yep. The guy is back, standing nonchalantly outside the door, his camera poised and ready at his hip. My heart sinks into my stomach.

"Let's go somewhere else. Maybe it's just a coincidence."

"Absolutely." Amanda abandons her underwear without a second thought, links her arm in mine, and walks me out of the shop.

We work very hard to keep up a conversation about absolutely nothing as we head down the street, and as soon as we turn the corner, we break into a run and duck into the nearest store, a big-chain costume jewelry shop. I duck behind a stand of earrings and peek outside.

Not ten seconds later, the guy in black comes around the corner, carefully looking into store windows as he walks. Amanda grabs my arm and hauls me to the back of the store, where we crouch down and pretend to look at a shelf of brightly printed scarves.

"What the fuck?" she mutters.

"I hate this. I'm so sorry," I murmur. "This isn't fair."

"Girl, you have no business apologizing! If that asshat out there thinks he's going to get some shots of you to sell, he's out of his damn mind. Do you want to go back to the car? We can drive somewhere else."

"No." I shake my head. "I'm sick of hiding from the fucking tabloids. What's the worst they can do, anyway? They've already tried to ruin everything and failed."

"Atta girl! Fuck him." Amanda laughs. Then she grows very serious. "Look. I'm ready to tell you my secret, but I need you to promise you won't judge."

"Um, obviously? Don't you know me better than that by now? This is a safe space."

"I know, I know. It's just..." She takes a breath. "Complicated." She takes another deep, steadying breath and then squeezes her eyes shut tight. "*Her name is Felicity.*"

For a second, I don't understand what she's telling me. And then suddenly, it all makes sense. The hesitation, the dodging questions, the avoidance, the worry. Everything clicks.

"You have to say something. Right now," Amanda says, eyes popping open, immediately looking sick. "I mean it, Abbie, you cannot leave me hanging here."

Instead of responding, I tackle her in a hug. Amanda shrieks a little, unstable in our crouched position, and we topple over. Everyone stares at us, but I don't care.

"Amanda, you little minx. This is amazing!" I gush. I help her to her feet and give her another hug. "You have to tell me all about her!"

"We met last semester in my writing elective. She's an English major. I didn't think anything of it at first, I've only ever been with guys, you know? But we hit it off and we've been texting all summer, just casually keeping in touch, and then a few weeks ago we started hanging out, and..." Amanda trails off, a smile on her face. "I haven't really mentioned her because I didn't want you to think there was someone creeping in on your best friend spot."

I shake my head. "Literally no one can take my place. Please."

"Right? Exactly!" She smiles widely. "So we've been going really slow because I told her I've never dated women before, but...it's the most amazing thing ever, Abbie. She has short black hair and all these tattoos and like, this whole down-for-whatever vibe. She loves to read. She took me out on a date for squid on a stick and then we rode a Ferris wheel and played boardwalk games until she won me this gigantic, like, stuffed animal donut with a face, which she named Bao. Which means treasure. Ha! God. She's so fun. I think you're gonna love her."

"I already do. And you know what? Fuck the camera guy. We're going back to Plume. I wanna help you look hot for your new girlfriend."

Amanda gives me a hug. "Thank you. You're the literal best."

I hug her back, thrilled that we've cleared the air between us and that we're not going to let some paparazzo ruin our day together.

As we walk out of the shop, arm in arm, my heart feels lighter than it has in days.

Chapter Twenty-Eight

Abbie

AFTER A LONG DAY of lunching and shopping and paparazzi ditching and boba tea-ing with Amanda, it's nice to be back at the estate with nothing on my agenda but to relax.

I give her the promised tour of the house first and then hug her goodbye before crawling into my bed and taking a two-hour nap. I manage to miss dinner completely, but it's worth it. I haven't slept a full night in longer than I can remember, and something about being with my best friend really set me at ease after these last few epically shitty weeks.

Not that there haven't been any bright spots, of course. But the whole Natasha thing has been casting a dark shadow over all of our lives, and I'm running out of encouraging things to tell Jude every time she asks me when her mom is going to wake up. Nobody knows the answer to that, not even the team of doctors tending to her. And the longer Natasha is unconscious, the worse her chances of a full recovery. I do know that much. I'll never say it to Jude, though.

I get up and change into a casual T-shirt dress, caught in that liminal space between evening and bedtime where putting together a real outfit seems pointless. Maybe I'll see if Graham wants to join me for a night swim, but first I need food. So I head down to the kitchen, hoping Mary packed up some leftovers for me to snack on.

What I find is lobster. Bow tie pasta salad with pesto, pine nuts, cherry tomatoes, and fresh basil. There's also garlic bread, grilled summer vegetables, thin sliced steak...plus creamy spinach dip and a layered dessert made with blueberries, strawberries, and pound cake. My God. It's a feast. More of Jude's favorites, I'm sure—she hasn't been eating much. I make a small plate and then sit at the island with it, thinking about how spoiled I've gotten while living here.

Things used to be like this at my house growing up. When my dad had money, we always had someone to cook our meals and clean up after us. Our house isn't as big as the estate, of course, and the staff size was considerably smaller and less frequent, but it was there. And then one day...they weren't. And then my dad started stressing about the mortgage and the bills and where exactly the rainy-day funds in the savings account had gone. My mom changed, too.

But being here at the Ratliff estate reminds me of being a kid again. In a good way. I feel...utterly taken care of. Safe. Secure. Everything I could ever possibly want is here, including Graham and Jude. The only thing that would make it any better is if Amanda could be here more often. Maybe I can talk to Graham about that. Maybe she can spend a few days here, hanging out with me and Jude. Having that tiny bit of my old life for these last few weeks would be so nice.

In my pocket, my phone vibrates. It's a text. From my dad.

I'm almost afraid to read it.

Someone should talk a little sense into Graham about unplugging that woman. Having his ex out of the picture for good certainly wouldn't hurt your case.

My body runs cold at the implication of his nasty text. Admittedly, he's not wrong about my situation being easier with Natasha permanently out of the way, but what a disgusting thing to say. I don't respond, just immediately delete the text. Fuck him.

I won't lie to myself and pretend my intentions were pure when I came here. My dad sent me here to seduce Graham, and then blackmail him or marry him, depending on the day. But I don't care what my dad wants anymore. I'm in love with Graham, and no matter what the universe throws at us, for better or worse, I want to build a life with him. And Jude, too.

As I pass by the living room, I hear the sound of the TV. Backing up, I step into the room to find Graham and Jude cozied up together on the couch. I pause in the doorway, hovering behind them, not wanting to interrupt the moment.

When I first got here, Graham barely even looked at Jude, much less spent time with her. And now they're here together, supporting each other during this ordeal, and it's the sweetest thing ever. Graham's had to work to earn himself small moments like this.

Jude suddenly turns around, and I realize she has tears dripping down her face.

"What's the matter?" I ask, walking over.

Graham drops a kiss on the top of her head and says, "She's worried about her mother."

"I'm scared," Jude warbles. "I want to go see her."

"Oh, sweetie." I drop onto the couch beside her and rub her back. "Visiting hours are over for the day. It's from ten to seven, remember? Maybe we can try to go tomorrow. "

I glance over at Graham and he nods.

"We'll go in the morning. I promise. I'll have Ronaldo drive us down first thing."

Jude nods, but her tears don't stop. "I want—her—to come home," she sobs haltingly.

"I know, sweetheart." Graham reaches for a box of tissues on the coffee table and sets them gently in Jude's lap. "And she'd be here if she could. But for now, she needs to stay where the doctors can take care of her. Once she's all better, she'll be home again."

"I—don't—believe you," Jude says to him, releasing a fresh wave of tears.

"What's all this, now?" Graham says gently, doing an excellent job of keeping the shock off his face. "Jude, why don't you believe me, love?"

Between sobs, she finally manages to get out, "Because I heard you say it before. Mommy's not coming back. You're moving all of her things back to New York!"

As Jude's meltdown continues, Graham says, "Ah. Well. I can understand you being upset about all of that."

"She's my *mom*," Jude stresses. "She should be here with me. I can take care of her!"

"She should be with you, yes. You're exactly right. But things are a little more complicated than that, Jude," Graham says soothingly.

"It's *not* complicated. You just have to keep her stuff here. And when she's all better, she'll come back, and we can be a family again," Jude says.

"Should I go? Give you some privacy?" I ask, suddenly very self-conscious. This isn't my business, no matter how badly I want it to be.

"Stay," Graham says quietly. "Jude, love, I'm sorry I haven't been more forward with you about all of this. I suppose I just...didn't want to upset you."

"Too late," she grumbles.

This makes Graham laugh, just a little. "You know, you can be surprisingly frank, just like your father. Sometimes I forget how much alike we can be."

That earns him a half-smile from Jude.

He takes her hand in his, dwarfing it and making her look impossibly smaller, and then goes on. "Your mother and I, we...we loved each other once, very much, but over time we grew apart. We wanted different things. We still loved each other but we started fighting, and we couldn't agree about anything, and we weren't able to be kind to one another anymore. We weren't happy together anymore."

"Yeah. I know," Jude says sadly. "Was it because of... because of me?"

"Oh, Jude. Look at me, love. No. We didn't split up because of you. We both love you with our whole hearts, and you were never something to fight about. We fought about completely different things, and we still do, because sometimes...well, sometimes grown-ups can't act properly around other certain types of grown-ups. We tried for a long time, Jude. We tried hard to fix things with us. It didn't work."

"But I want us all to be together." Jude's lower lip trembles. "Like a real family."

"We *are* a real family," Graham insists. "We're still your mum and dad, and you're our little girl. That will never change. But your mother and I can't live in the same house and be happy that way. Which is why it's better for us, and for you, when she and I live apart. So as soon as she's out of the hospital, she'll be moving back into her place in Manhattan. And you and I will be down there at my apartment during your school year as well. We'll be just across town from each other, and you'll be able to see her every day if you want."

"Why can't she just come back here? I like it better here. She could stay in my room. You wouldn't even have to talk to each other," Jude pleads desperately.

My heart breaks for her a thousand times over.

Graham clears his throat, and I see his eyes getting damp. "Your mother needs to be in New York City for work, love. This place is too far away. And she loves the city. It makes her happy. Just like being here, as much as I can, makes me happy. You understand that, don't you?"

Jude sniffles, thinking it over, but I see her soften against her father. "I'm still sad."

"That's okay," Graham reassures her. "It's okay to be sad. It might take a while before you start to feel better about it, and that's okay, too. We won't stop loving you because you're sad."

"What if I'm mad, too?" she asks.

Graham smiles. "We'll still love you, no matter how you feel."

She glances over at me, brows knitted together, and I give her knee a squeeze to let her know I'm here for her, too.

"How about I put you to bed tonight?" he offers. "It's about that time, and I'm getting tired, too. I heard Abbie's been reading you *Black Beauty*. I could read you a chapter or two?"

She seems to give it some serious consideration before saying, "Okay."

Graham shoots me a wink and gets up off the couch, extending a formal hand to Jude. She gives me a hug to say good night first, and I can't help swooning as I watch them leave the room hand in hand.

He really is going to be a great dad. He just needs the opportunity and the skills, the patience and the time, and I'm here to help with all of the above.

I can help them grow together into something beautiful.

Chapter Twenty-Nine

Abbie

AMANDA IS TEXTING me pictures of her and Felicity on their date at an old-fashioned ice cream parlor when Graham comes back into the living room almost an hour later. I tuck my phone away and watch him cross the room.

"How'd it go with Jude?" I ask.

"She's still struggling, but I think the talk was good for her. Well. I hope it was. She has some answers now, even if she doesn't necessarily like them." He drops onto the couch beside me and lightly runs his hands down my arms, his gaze intensifying. "I wanted to say thank you."

My skin starts to tingle under the heat of his touch. "For what?"

"For your presence in my home." He squeezes my shoulders, sending a shiver down my spine. "There's no way to say this that doesn't sound trite, but Abbie, you make me...*better*. A better person. A better father. The relationship I have with Jude now, the one I'm working every day to build, is in direct correlation to your presence in my life. You...elevate me."

Butterflies doesn't even begin to cover it. In this moment, I feel like I could fly.

"You've had all of that inside of you this whole time, Graham. I just helped you see it."

"No." He shakes his head firmly. "I've been a bloody cunt for a long time. It's only because of you pushing me that I'm finally changing. So tonight, I want to thank you for that."

"Oh really?" I say teasingly. "In that case, I accept. I do love the way you say thank you."

He cups the back of my head and kisses me, softly at first, stirring the spark of want in my stomach, until he probes my lips open with his tongue and I nearly lose myself. I follow his lead, my favorite thing to do, and soon enough we're horizontal, both of us moaning quietly.

"Shouldn't we go someplace more private?" I whisper, pulling back.

He sits up, reaching down to me to tuck a strand of hair behind my ear. "I'll do you one better. Will you allow me to steal you away for a romantic evening? It's the least you deserve."

"Maybe. What did you have in mind?" I skid my palm up the inside of his thigh and take delight in the way he growls.

"It's a secret. You'll just have to trust me." Graham digs around in his pocket and pulls out a blindfold. He shifts me to a sitting position, and I let him slide it gently over my eyes. "Is this okay?"

I can't see a thing, but I offer a smile and a nod even

though I'm shaking on the inside. There is something so vulnerable and terrifying and yet completely delightful about this.

Graham kisses me again, his firm lips skating against mine, his fingers tracing a line down the center of my back, and my heightened senses somehow take it to another level. I've kissed him in the dark plenty of times, but this feels different. The power of his touch and his tongue are magnified under the blindfold. He takes my hand and guides me to my feet, then carefully leads me down the hall. I'm grateful the estate is so massive, with its wide halls and generously sized rooms. I have no fear of knocking anything over or walking into a wall.

"Where are we going?" I ask. "Can I have a hint?"

He just laughs, and then I realize we've reached the stairs. I guess we're not leaving the estate? As we begin our slow ascent, one step at a time, I start to notice the low sounds of music coming from the floor above. There are no lyrics, just guitar, bass, violin—it's old jazz.

"Django Reinhardt," I say with a smile. "My grandpa loved this music."

"A man of excellent taste," Graham says. "It must run in your family."

I know he's teasing me, but sudden thoughts of my father threaten to ruin my date before it's even begun. Luckily, I'm distracted by the smell of something sweet and smoky, sandalwood with a hint of vanilla maybe, and I feel the flooring change beneath my feet from hardwood to plush carpet. The music is getting louder, though it's still fairly muted. I think we're in Graham's bedroom, which quickens my pulse because I know what happens in this bedroom. And I'm *starving* for it. But we keep going.

The floor changes again, to tile, our footsteps echoing around us in the space. Beneath the sound of the jazz, I hear the heavy click of Graham closing a door behind us, and then we come to a stop. He kisses me tenderly and gently pulls the blindfold off my eyes. "Welcome."

We're in his expansive marble bathroom, dim and warmly glowing with the light of what must be a hundred candles in glass jars of all shapes and sizes. The clawfoot tub in the middle of the room is frothing with bubbles, and a small cart sitting beside it holds two flutes of cham- pagne and gold-edged dishes of fruit and fancy choco- lates and Chantilly cream and tiny, delicately adorned cakes. The French doors that open onto the balcony are wide open, showing off an indigo sky full of twinkling stars and a soft yellow moon.

I spin around slowly, taking it all in.

"This is amazing," I whisper.

"You are amazing." Graham moves in front of me and takes my hands in his, gazing into my eyes. "And I am so lucky to have you in my life."

"I don't even know what to say."

"You don't have to say anything." He kisses the tips of my fingers. "This is my night to take care of you."

Forget bubbles, I'm basically a melted puddle with a heartbeat. Graham slowly undresses me, his fingertips sending delicious bolts of electricity through me as he carefully pulls off my cotton dress and trails his fingers down my bra straps. I move to help him take it off, but he stills my hand.

"Shh. Let me undress you," he says, quiet and intense.

I bite my lip and nod. It's so warm in here, yet I have goosebumps all over.

He has me naked in seconds, dropping kisses over my bare skin, his firm hands squeezing my ass just the way I like. Between the jazz and the candles and his hands on me and the luscious scent of bubbles, I'm completely overwhelmed. In the best way possible.

When he gently sucks on my earlobe, I feel my knees go weak. Letting out a moan, I wrap my arms around his neck and sag against him. This is magic. Kissing me the whole time, he leads me to the bathtub step by step and then spins me around and helps me into it. The water is the perfect temperature—not too hot, but warm enough to make me hiss with pleasure as I sink to the bottom, relishing the feel of the bubbles against my skin. Graham kneels next to the tub and kisses my shoulder.

"You're not getting in?" I ask.

"I'm taking care of you tonight, remember?" The way he says it, his hand slipping under the water to squeeze my inner thigh, sends lightning straight to my core.

Graham bathing me is an experience in and of itself. His hands are so strong, so sure, and as he strokes me from neck to toe with a soft bath puff, I realize how *cared for* I feel with him. I feel appreciated, treasured...adored, even.

He begins washing my hair, which feels like heaven, and then rinses with fresh water before massaging conditioner into my scalp. His fingers move slow, firmly, circling in little spirals until I'm gasping. I didn't know bathing someone could be so erotic, but my blood is pumping and my center is white-hot.

I let him finish with my hair before leaning over to cup his face in my hands.

"Graham." As I search his eyes, I feel the urge to pour out my heart to him right now, to actually say the words I've been dying to say to him out loud. But I hesitate. I'm scared of pushing him away. Scared of being too needy, too hungry. Too open. Too vulnerable.

I kiss him fiercely instead, trying to telegraph what I'm feeling. Hoping I can work up the nerve to give this emotion voice.

"Abbie," he murmurs against my mouth, and the way he says my name pushes me over the edge. I need him. I need all of him.

Climbing out of the tub, I seat myself on his lap, heedless of the water I'm getting all over his clothes and the floor. He laughs and wraps his arms around my wet, naked body, our kiss softening to something sweet and gentle. One that steals my words entirely.

"Abbie," he says again, breathlessly, a note of urgency in his voice this time.

"Mmm," I moan, feeling his cock straining in his pants. I grind against him, already tugging at his belt. "Take me to bed. Dessert can wait. I want you now."

"No." He suddenly pulls back, panting for air, looking into my eyes with an intensity I've never seen before.

"No what? Dessert...can't wait?" I ask, laughing a little.

"No, I—I have to tell you something first," he says. "I have to tell you that...I love you."

The whole world stops. There's not a single doubt in my mind that he's telling the truth. I feel it instantly, in my bones, warm and strong. This man loves me.

But Graham seems to mistake my initial shock for disbelief.

"I've loved you for a long time," he rushes on, "I just wouldn't let myself admit it. I thought it was too messy. I thought it was a midlife crisis. I thought about a lot of things, but I don't bloody care anymore, Abbie. I don't care what it is because I know it to be truer than anything else I've ever known. I'm unstoppably, undeniably, desperately in love with you. My heart beats your name in my chest. There is no one else for me on this earth. I love you."

I shake my head and laugh, so filled with wonder and joy that I can barely speak.

"You infuriating, beautiful man. I love you too," I tell him simply. "I always have."

The look on his face could break my heart if it wasn't so deeply happy. We collide again, fumbling with his clothes, popping buttons, slipping on the floor, both of us a wet, laughing mess as we tumble into the bedroom, and we don't care. We don't care because we are in love and there is nothing, nothing in the whole world, that matters more than this.

Chapter Thirty

Graham

ABBIE COMES HARD AND FAST, her wet hair slapping against my chest, my finger deep inside her clenched asshole. As she curses and moans, riding out the final, shuddering waves, I force myself to hold back. Past experience tells me she'll be ready for another round in minutes.

"That was delicious," she sighs, collapsing on the bed beside me. "I haven't had a good bath in a long time."

My cock is still rock hard and throbbing and slick with her juices, my balls tight with longing. I take a steadying breath. "That's a shame. We can arrange more of them, if you like."

I trace circles around her pebbled nipples, captivated by how erect they are.

"I very much like. And I like this, too."

She climbs back on top of me, lowering her breast until it's a hairsbreadth from my mouth.

"Naughty girl," I murmur, flicking her nipple with my tongue.

She arcs a brow and grins down at me. "Suck me," she commands, running a hand through my hair and then tugging a little. "You're supposed to be taking care of me tonight, remember?"

"I remember."

I wrap my mouth around her nipple and suck it into my mouth hungrily, rolling my tongue over it, pressing gently with my teeth until she's panting. Then I take my turn with her other breast, feeling the wetness leak from her cunt onto my abs. Before I'm even done, she's backing away from me, inching down my body until my cock brushes her vulva. This girl has little self-control when it comes to sex. It's something I've always enjoyed about her.

Grabbing her hips, I hold her still as I plunge into her once again, warming her back up with a series of short, rapid thrusts. Abbie slams herself back in perfect time with my pumping, her mouth falling open, her eyes going half-lidded. Soon enough I'm lengthening each glide, thrusting deeper and harder, plunging new depths, both of us groaning at the delicious friction.

"Think you can try to keep it down this time?" I tease. "The jazz isn't quite loud enough to drown out your screams."

"With a man as sexy as you, it's hard to keep quiet."

"Now you're playing to my ego," I growl. "Careful."

"I know you like it. I know exactly what you like." She leans in and sucks my earlobe.

With a desperate moan, I pull out of her and rock us to a sitting position. "Get on your hands and knees. I'm going to positively ravish you, Miss Montgomery."

She obeys quickly, wiggling her tight, round ass at me, looking over her shoulder to say, "Don't make promises you can't keep, Mr. Ratliff."

"I am a man of my word."

I dive back into her from behind, squeezing her ass cheeks and ramming her like some kind of wild animal. Nothing is holding me back, and I can't get enough.

"Oh fuck," Abbie moans. "Fuck yes. Oh *yes.*"

It would be easy enough for both of us to come right now—I can feel it, getting closer by the second—but I have a powerful urge to devour her like she's the last treacle tart and I'm starving. I positively crave the taste of her sweet cunt on my tongue. Denying myself for the second time tonight, I pull out, instructing Abbie to lay on her back with her legs spread wide.

I stand over her and take in an eyeful as I catch my breath, savoring the vision of her supple naked body on my sheets. This is a view I could never get used to. The moonlight spilling across her smooth skin, the curve of her hips, the dip of her lower belly, those pert, perfect tits.

"Beautiful," I murmur. There's no other word for her.

Climbing onto the bed, I find her pussy ready and waiting for me, slick with arousal. I push her thighs apart even wider and lick her from top to bottom, then back up again, the taste of her like ripe fruit lingering on my tongue as I make another pass. Her moans are like fingers curling around my cock and squeezing, stealing my breath as I reach her clit.

I've always prided myself on my oral skills, but Abbie makes me feel like a god. Every flick of my tongue sends her shivering and moaning. Every gentle nibble of her clit makes her writhe against me, thrusting her cunt against my mouth. I eagerly oblige her, lavishing her center with broad strokes. Her fingers twine in my hair, pulling to the point of pain as I get her closer to the edge. I could spend an eternity doing this to her.

She feels like my life force. Every lick, every moan that spills out of her, is something I could live on forever. I slip a finger into her opening and feel her walls tighten, and as I slide back and forth, faster and faster, fucking her with my finger as hard as I'm licking her with my mouth, Abbie moans my name. Over and over. She's begging me to stop before she comes. But I won't quit until I taste her orgasm on my tongue.

Her thighs squeeze the sides of my head, her nails clawing at my scalp, but I don't let up until her body convulses and she cries out, grinding hard against my face. She's so loud, she'd wake the entire house if we were still in New York. Luckily, we're here in my expansive home, able to be as loud as we want, and the knowledge that I don't have to hide her anymore is just as much an aphrodisiac as the scent of her sex.

I place kisses up her body as I scale her like a mountain. She's still shivering and moaning, coming down from her high, but she grabs for me like she can't get enough. No woman has ever craved me like this, has wanted *me*. They want the things around me, the wealth and status, the perks of being on my arm. I've been merely secondary. Not with Abbie.

"You're so good," she moans softly. "Damn, you're so good."

I laugh softly and suck on her left nipple, pleased to

see her arch her back as I do.

"There is little I love more than your body." I move to the right nipple. "It's practically a religious experience."

She giggles. "Does that make you some kind of monk, then?"

"It might. Up for a little role play, are we?" I give her nipple a quick bite and she sucks in a deep breath. "I know you like it a little rough."

"I like all of it with you." She wiggles her body under me, getting impatient. "Get on your back. It's my turn to suck you off."

Oh, the way her sweet mouth says such filthy words. There are just so many things to love about her, including her eagerness to give head. But right now, I only want to be inside her and cradle her to me, feel her skin against my skin, her heartbeat thudding against mine. I crave that touch more than my dick in her mouth. There will be plenty of nights left for kinky sex, for rough sex, for role play, even.

Tonight is for making love. For communicating the depth of my feelings in all the ways my words cannot express. In all the ways I still don't understand.

"Let me make you come again first," I tell her. "Don't make me beg."

"Your wish is my command," she whispers.

I plunge into her and she takes me in eagerly, moaning happily with every thrust. We kiss away our pain, our fear, our relentless hunger for each other, the grief of our recent separation, and it reinvigorates my soul.

"Pull my hair," she murmurs against me. "Spank me."

I almost come at her demands. "Naughty girl."

"So treat me like one," she begs. "Leave your mark on me."

I oblige. I push her onto her knees again, this time on the floor, her face pressed into the rug, and fuck her hard from behind. Then I use her long hair as a leash and fuck her even harder, until my eyes nearly cross.

"More," she demands. I've never felt her get so wet before.

I smack her ass as hard as I dare, again and again, getting rougher as she eggs me on, finally agreeing to dole out a single whip with my belt before massaging the sting away and entering her again. I pump into her gently, kissing her back, fondling her pert little hole.

"I can't keep this up much longer," I tell her, my voice thick with the strain. "I've been holding back all night. I'm going to fucking explode inside that cunt."

"Don't hold back. Get loud for me," Abbie begs. "I love the sound of you turned on."

Together, our voices echo off the walls and furniture. She climaxes again, so loud I think she might wake the staff, and for some reason this gets me even more excited. The tightness expands to my balls and I know I'm done for, so I flip her onto her back and wrap my hand around her throat, telling her I love her one last time as I plunge back into her and let myself go.

Our eyes lock, and suddenly it's happening, the orgasm rushing at me in waves, one after the other, increasing in intensity, pushing me higher and higher. I'm suspended for a stretched-out moment, falling, flying. It's fucking endless. I've never felt anything like it before.

And then I start to gush deep inside her, euphoric warmth radiating through my body as I spill my seed, the force of it taking my breath away. I'm coming so hard my toes curl and my vision flickers.

As we fall asleep, I imagine fucking her on every surface in the estate. Bending her over the kitchen island again, finally giving myself permission to come all over that pretty face. On the stairs. In the stables. Can you fuck on the back of a horse? I'd like to find out. I drift off sometime around two or three a.m., with Abbie tucked comfortably in my arms and my soul at ease. Because this is the woman I'm going to spend the rest of my life with.

Too soon, I'm ripped from sleep by a loud banging. I stir, trying to make sense of the noise, when Esmeralda's voice cuts through the darkness.

"You can't go in there!"

Confused, I sit up just as the bedroom door goes flying open. Cops in dark blue uniforms flood my bedroom. Someone turns the lights on and Abbie awakens, startled, pulling the sheet up around her naked body.

"What is the meaning of this?" I demand, voice thick with sleep.

"Graham Ratliff, you are under arrest for the attempted murder of Natasha Ratliff," the one nearest to me says harshly.

"What?" Abbie cries out, shock written across her face.

"Sir, if you don't get up, we'll have to use force. You do not want to resist arrest."

"Give me a moment," I growl, now wide awake.

They don't leave the room to let me get decent, so I

grab my pants from the floor and slide them on. Meanwhile, Abbie looks like she's trying to shrink away from the world, curling up near the headboard with a pillow to her chest. I have to take charge of this situation.

I get out of bed and pull on the rest of my clothes. The officers wait until my final button is in place to cuff me. After the fat one finishes rattling off my Miranda rights, I turn to Abbie.

"Protect Jude," I tell her. "At all costs. Don't let anyone get near her, do you understand?"

Abbie just stares at me, face still frozen in horror. Then she nods slowly as the officer jerks my arm and hauls me out of the room, away from my love. Away from my child. Away from my home.

Graham and Abbie's story concludes in The Billionaire and His Forever...

We were always going to be an impossible fantasy.

There was never a future for us between the secrets and the scandals, the temptations and the lies, and above all--a child who never deserved this life.

But even when we hurt each other the most, when the entire world is rooting against us, when we've been betrayed and wrecked and somehow survived it all... how could we ever let go of this imperfect forever?

Find out what happens in The Billionaire and

His Forever.

Paige Press

Paige Press isn't just Laurelin Paige anymore...

Laurelin Paige has expanded her publishing company to bring readers even more hot romances.

Sign up for our newsletter to get the latest news about our releases and receive a free book from one of our amazing authors:

Laurelin Paige
Stella Gray
CD Reiss
Jenna Scott
Raven Jayne
JD Hawkins
Poppy Dunne
Lia Hunt
Sadie Black

Also by Sadie Black

HIS NANNY TRILOGY

The Billionaire and His Nanny

The Billionaire and His Scandal

The Billionaire and His Forever

About the Author

Sadie Black lives in her head as an ex-member of the British royal family, a current fashion icon, and couldn't be more annoyed that she has to pay taxes on a job called "governess."

Printed in Great Britain
by Amazon

10331455R00164